Praise for *The Final Hunt*

"A twisty thriller that stretches to the far reaches of the Alaskan tundra, The Final Hunt is a one-sit read, and Cameron Prescott is the kind of take-no-prisoners protagonist you'll be rooting for to the final, spine-tingling pages."

—**Danielle Girard,** *USA Today and* **Amazon #1 Bestselling Author**

"Audrey J. Cole's *THE FINAL HUNT* is a breathtaking thriller set in the frozen landscape of Alaska. It's populated by fascinating characters and full of shocking, long-buried secrets. Relentlessly paced and intriguing, this is the white-hot read of the summer."

—**David Bell,** *USA Today* **bestselling author of** *THE FINALISTS*

"Dark secrets lie at the heart of this riveting tale of murder and betrayal. The Final Hunt hooked me on the first page and didn't let go."

—**Chris Patchell,** *USA Today* **bestselling author**

"I love dark-edged thrillers that take place in snowy settings and keep me guessing. The Final Hunt delivers on all counts, and I devoured every page. Make hot tea, grab a blanket, and settle in to enjoy Audrey J. Cole's l̲ it. Fans of Lucey Foley's The

— ‖‖‖‖‖‖‖‖‖‖‖‖‖ stselling author
D1225668

Also By Audrey J. Cole

EMERALD CITY THRILLERS

THE RECIPIENT

INSPIRED BY MURDER

THE SUMMER NANNY

VIABLE HOSTAGE

FATAL DECEPTION

THE FERRY KILLER (Coming 2023)

BOOKS 1-5 BOX SET

STANDALONES

THE PILOT'S DAUGHTER

THE FINAL HUNT

AUDREY J. COLE

RAINIER
PUBLISHING

ISBN: 978-1-7373-6071-1

The Final Hunt

Cover by Rainier Book Design
RainierBookDesign.com
Cover photo by Creative Travel Projects @Shutterstock

Man is not what he thinks he is, he is what he hides.

–André Malraux

PROLOGUE

Simon bent over, placing his hands on his knees when he reached the top of the peak. He tried to find his breath as he looked beyond the tree line and scanned the valley below for the small airstrip and John's plane. The wind had picked up during Simon's frantic trek through the wilderness from where he'd last seen John, and the snow flurries whipped against his face.

You're almost there. Just a little farther. The airstrip was several miles closer to their hunting spot than the lodge where they were staying, but the hike had still taken him nearly two hours.

Sweat dripped into his eyes despite the freezing temperature. He stood up tall and forced his exhausted leg muscles to move down the slope. He took only a few steps before his legs propelled him faster than he could control, sending him face-down into the snow-covered ground between the trees.

"Ahh!"

Pain burned through his abdomen where his body skid atop a rock. He summoned what was left of his adrenaline to pull himself to his feet. Simon gripped the shoulder strap of his hunting rifle and took it slower the rest of the way down, ignoring the burn in his legs. When he reached the clearing, his heart beat rapidly against his ribs. A few inches of snow covered John's yellow Cessna, which remained the only plane parked at the secluded airstrip.

He covered the final few hundred yards as fast as his body allowed. He knew the plane was locked but tried the door handle anyway. Turning his face away from the side window, he hurled the butt of his rifle against the Plexiglass. The window fractured with a resounding *crack* amidst the quiet forest.

Simon threw his rifle into the window again, this time breaking through the acrylic. He reached through the broken shards and lifted the lock before swinging the door open and climbing inside. Somehow, it seemed colder in the plane than outside, but he tore off his hat and gloves, eyeing the radio.

He flipped the red master switch on the instrument panel. Lights illuminated across the controls. Static came through the headset when he pulled it on. With a trembling hand, he pulled the mouthpiece to his lips. Blood trickled down his wrist from where he'd scraped his arm when he reached through the broken window.

Simon pushed the small button on the yoke, readying himself.

"I have an emergency! Can anyone hear me?"

His breath filled the fuselage with puffs of white as he waited for a response.

A crackle came through his headset. "This is Super Cub five-six-Charlie. I read you. What's your emergency?"

Simon lowered his head and exhaled into the mouthpiece. "Oh, thank God."

"Repeat. What's your emergency?"

"I'm in the Frank Church Wilderness. My friend—" his voice broke. Simon swallowed hard and continued. "We were out deer hunting. The guy I'm with was attacked by a bear. A couple of them. About six miles from here."

"Okay, I follow you. I need your location."

"I already told you! We're in the Frank Church Wilderness."

"I understand. But *where* in the Frank Church Wilderness? Are you in the air, or on the ground?"

"I'm not a pilot—I'm in my friend's plane." Simon looked beyond the shattered side window to his right. He squinted to read the sign beside the windsock. "We're parked at the Big Creek airstrip."

"Roger that. Are you with your friend now?"

"No! I told you, he's six miles away!"

"I need you to keep calm, sir. Is he wounded? What's his condition?"

"Um…." Simon thought of the blood that covered John's hunting pack. There were signs of a fight in the snow surrounding it, and John's gun abandoned on the ground. "It's bad, I know that. We were working a ridge, driving deer, walking a couple hundred feet apart. I heard him yell out, like

9

he was in trouble. When I got closer, I saw two bears. I fired at the big one, and I think I hit her, but it didn't slow her down. They took off down a ravine. I shouted for John and heard him scream again—farther away. I headed down the hill and followed the bear tracks to a creek. There was even more blood than where they first got him. I went up and down that creek, calling out his name, looking for blood, or if they dragged him up the other bank. But there was nothing." His voice wobbled before a sob escaped his throat.

"Okay, hang in there. I'll relay that information to the authorities. Help should be there in an hour or so."

"An hour!"

"Well, I'm guessing the rescue will come out of Boise from the Air National Guard."

"All right then, just call them! And hey…thank you."

"To save your battery, you'll want to turn your master switch off for the next forty-five minutes. Then get back on this frequency, and the rescue team will contact you when they're getting close. Got that?"

"I got it."

"One last thing. What's your name? What kind of plane you in?"

"Simon Castelli. I'm in a yellow Cessna. It's the only plane here!"

"You're pretty far out there. Hold tight, stay out of the wind, and hydrate. The rescue team's going to want you with them when they head out to look for your friend."

"But there's not a lot of light left."

"Yeah, I know. But if you can point out where you last saw your friend, it's going to help. You going to be up for that? Are you injured at all?"

Simon rubbed his aching ribs. Tucked inside his coat, he felt the flask John had given him just yesterday to celebrate the trip. Full of Macallan 25-year single malt Scotch.

"I'll be fine. But tell them to hurry—no one's going to last long out there."

CHAPTER ONE

Three Months Later

Cameron watched the light snow fall outside her cabin and wondered if any of her husband's remains were still out there. She twisted the stem of her glass between her fingers and turned from the window. The photos from their honeymoon remained on the screen of her laptop. She moved across the cozy room and stopped at the knotty pine bookshelf, buying time before she returned to her ritual of poring over old photographs while consuming too much wine.

She ran her hand across the spines of John's books. There was some fiction, but the shelf was mainly filled with big-game hunting and outdoor guides. Although John had been a prominent criminal defense attorney—arguably the best in the Pacific Northwest—there wasn't a single law book in sight.

John kept long hours and would often work around the clock when preparing for a trial. This cabin, however, was his retreat from it all. When John was alive, the cabin was always more of *his* place. She joined him on occasional weekend trips, but she preferred life in the city.

Since he died, she'd been coming to the cabin, nestled in the North Cascades, every weekend. And sometimes it felt like he was still here.

Cameron's hand stopped on an elk hunting guide. She pulled the well-worn book from the shelf when something clattered lightly atop the hardwood floor beside her bare feet. She laid the book on the shelf and reached down to pick up the small plastic case, surprised to see it contained an SD card.

The SD cards that she'd brought from their home were from a drawer in John's office. Like everything of John's, they'd been meticulously organized, sorted by the dates the photos were taken. She'd been looking through those same photos over and over for these last three months.

She smiled, thinking of him toting his fancy camera around his neck on all their vacations. She clutched the card in her palm and wondered what old memories were captured in these pictures, waiting to be revisited now. She crossed the room and sat on the worn-out couch beside the dwindling fire in the wood stove.

After taking a large drink of her Merlot, she set the glass on the coffee table among the array of SD cards she'd brought with her for the weekend. Before removing the memory card from her laptop, she paused on a photo of her and John holding up a blue marlin on a chartered fishing boat in Mexico, and laughed.

John had convinced her to go with him on the fishing trip, even though she'd wanted to stay back and lie by the pool. Fishing was never her thing, but she agreed to go along and spend the day with him. She'd reeled in the marlin after only having her line in the water for a few minutes. It was so big John had to help her hold it for the photo. John fished the entire rest of the day without catching a thing. They'd joked about her out-fishing him for years afterward. At least he was smart enough to never ask her to go fishing with him again.

Cameron pulled out the little card and replaced it with the one in her hand.

Her therapist warned her about spending all her weekends up here. Alone. She told Cameron it was unhealthy for her to keep digging up old memories with a bottle of wine instead of going out with friends and making new ones. That it was keeping her from moving on. Living.

But not yet. That would come.

She opened the contents of the memory card, glad to see there were hundreds of photos. Cameron hardly ever took pictures. It was always John. She clicked on the tiny thumbnail of the first image, which was nothing but a blur of darkness.

She plucked her wineglass from the coffee table and went to the next. The photo was of a woman Cameron didn't recognize leaving a coffee shop; she looked away from the camera, as if unaware of her photo being taken.

Cameron's stomach sank. These were all photos John had stored from some case, taken by his private investigator. There were no new photos of them.

The next photo showed the dark-haired woman getting out of a white SUV. Again, her eyes were diverted from the camera. The photos reminded Cameron of paparazzi stalking a celebrity. She felt an uneasiness creep over her and took a full sip from her wine.

She clicked through several more photos of the same woman. Jogging. Shopping. In all of them, she appeared oblivious of the photographer.

The next photo sent goosebumps down Cameron's limbs and to the top of her scalp. Despite the fire crackling next to her, the cabin suddenly felt cold. The same woman was now obviously deceased.

She lay on her back. Naked. Her skin mottled and a marbled gray. Her lips were a bluish purple, and her eyes were closed. Severe bruising lined her neck. Cameron put a hand over her mouth and clicked to the next photo. It was of the same woman, only zoomed out.

The woman was lying on a bed. Her skin looked even more ashen next to the red bedspread. Cameron looked away and racked her brain for why John would have had these photos. Maybe he'd gotten them from a client he defended. Though it was unlike him to keep evidence like this lying loosely inside his bookshelf.

Cameron clicked to the next photo. She gasped as her glass slipped from her fingers and shattered on the wood floor between her feet.

She stared at the hand-carved cedar bedframe the dead woman was lying on. It was the same bed Cameron had slept in last night. A shirtless man stood at the end of the bed, his reflection captured in the photo by a large mirror above the headboard. He was looking down at the dead woman, and he aimed his black Nikon toward her for the photo.

Cameron recognized the man immediately. She'd know that face anywhere. It was the face she'd been missing and grieving over for the last three months. It was John.

CHAPTER TWO

Cameron stared at the detective as he studied his laptop screen. She took a sip from the Styrofoam cup of coffee the tall detective had given her, grateful to be seated across from him so she wouldn't have to see the photos again. After her initial catatonic shock last night, the reality of seeing John standing over a dead woman's body had sunk in. She'd skimmed through the rest of the photos and had found there were at least seven victims.

Having had no cell service and too much wine, Cameron had to wait until dawn to drive over Snoqualmie Pass to deliver the photos to the Seattle Police Headquarters, which was only a few blocks from John's old law firm. She'd tossed and turned all night on the couch, unable to step foot in the bedroom where the dead woman lay in John's photographs. After she'd told the officer at the front desk that she had photographic evidence to several murders, the sandy-haired detective met her in the lobby and introduced himself as Tanner Mulholland. He then brought her to a small windowless room on the seventh floor. He referred to it as *the soft room.*

While the detective assured her she'd done the right thing by coming in, he didn't seem as surprised by the evidence as she'd expected. Although, unlike her, she told herself, they dealt with this sort of thing every day. And John wasn't *his* late husband. But still.

Finally, he closed the laptop and folded his hands atop the table between them. Cameron felt nauseous from the bitter coffee on her empty stomach and the bottle of wine she'd polished off last night. The shock of these photos was worse than John never returning from his hunting trip. It felt like he had died all over again.

When the detective looked at her, she willed him to tell her that she had made a mistake. That the man in the photos wasn't John. That they had already caught the person who killed these women. Someone who looked like John, but not him. Someone John represented, which is why he had these disturbing images.

The detective's intelligent eyes met hers.

"Did you ever suspect your husband was killing women?"

Cameron stiffened in her chair. She had come prepared to talk to the police, but not like this. "No. Of course not."

He let her statement linger in the air.

"I'm mortified—heartbroken." Couldn't he see how upset she was?

"Do you know who any of these women were?"

She shook her head. "No."

"They were victims of The Teacher Killer." His voice was calm.

Cameron wanted to scream. "The *Teacher Killer*?"

He nodded.

Cameron knew from the excessive news coverage of the grotesque nature of the Teacher Killings. The victims were raped and tortured before they were strangled. Afterward, their killer used a knife to inscribe a grade, ranging from A to F, on their lower backs. The more they fought back, the better grade they received.

"I thought the Teacher Killer victims were all murdered in their own homes?"

"The ones whose bodies we found were, because they all lived alone. But two teachers went missing a year and a half ago, one from Eagle High School and the other from Queen Anne Heights. They were both married; one of them had children. I have always believed them to be victims of the Teacher Killer, even though we haven't found their bodies. And now, one of them appears to be the deceased woman in the photos taken at your cabin."

Cameron felt the room start to spin.

"I've been building a case against your late husband for the last six months, and I was close to having enough to arrest him when he was killed in the hunting accident. Although, most of the evidence up until that point was circumstantial. Being a criminal defense attorney, John was good at covering his tracks. Until his last victim scratched him before he killed her, leaving a trace of his DNA under her fingernails."

Cameron gripped the seat of her padded folding chair.

"John's DNA wasn't in the system when I ran the DNA evidence through our database. But there was a case nearly thirty years ago that shared many similarities to the more recent teacher killings. I learned the victim, Bethany Valdez, had been John's ninth-grade substitute English teacher, which was what first led me to suspect him."

Cameron threw her hand up, wanting him to stop.

"I'm sorry. I tested the blood that was found on John's hunting gear where he disappeared against some old evidence from that case along with the DNA from his last victim—the West Seattle teacher who was killed last summer. The results came back yesterday. They're a match."

Cameron felt like she'd had the wind knocked out of her. *The police knew?*

It was true. "So, John killed more women than the ones in the photos?" Her voice came out a croak.

The detective nodded once. "I'll add these photos to the other evidence we've compiled, but we will be posthumously charging John with the murders of *eleven* women."

Her vision blurred when Detective Mulholland stood from his chair. He reached out for her arm across the table.

"Cameron?" she heard him say, before everything went black.

CHAPTER THREE

Cameron sat in the front seat of Mulholland's black Ford. The detective had insisted on driving her home after she'd passed out at the homicide unit. He informed her that he had a warrant to search her Laurelhurst house, their Cle Elum cabin, and even their airplane hangar to ensure John hadn't been keeping evidence that could lead to other victims.

She closed her eyes as he turned onto her narrow street.

"You okay?"

It seemed like a stupid question for a detective. Of course she wasn't okay.

"I mean, do you feel like you're going to pass out again?" he asked, as if reading her thoughts.

She exhaled and looked out the window. "I'll be fine."

He'd already offered to call someone to be with her for support, but she declined. Her parents were gone now. Her only friends were her office employees, and she wasn't ready to face them.

The homes on her street were a mix of new and old, varying styles, all with immaculate yards and views of Lake

Washington. Detective Mulholland appeared to be taking in the neatly trimmed hedges and shrubbery, rose gardens, and imported palm trees that lined the street.

"Nice part of the city," the detective observed.

Cameron knew immediately what he meant. None of this beauty mattered now.

When he pulled to a stop next to the wrought-iron gate in front of her white Tudor, there was a CSI van already parked on the street in front of them. Across the street was a black SUV with government plates. She got out of the car and saw her neighbors across the street, the Parkers, standing outside on their porch, casually observing the scene at Cameron's house. She didn't bother to wave. Neither did they.

Cameron counted four people get out of the CSI van before she followed Mulholland up the paved steps to her blue front door. He glanced at clematis crawling up the side of the porch. She let him in, followed by the team of crime scene investigators.

She watched the investigators don latex gloves and waste no time dispersing through her home to search her private things. Her front door opened without so much as a knock and Cameron turned to see two men wearing suits let themselves into her home. One was overweight with white hair and the younger, muscular man reminded her of Mark Wahlberg.

Mulholland introduced them to Cameron as a sergeant and a detective, whose names escaped her as soon as they rolled off Mulholland's tongue. He had already explained that she could be present while they conducted their search but would remain under the supervision of a detective until they were done. As she watched a woman pull her wedding dishes out from the antique china hutch, she'd had enough.

"I'll wait outside."

Mulholland turned from the built-in bookshelf he was looking through. "It's going to be awhile."

"That's okay. I can't watch this."

With the muscular detective on her heels, Cameron went to the kitchen and poured a glass of water before walking out the French doors at the rear of her home. The patio chair was wet from that morning's rain when she sat down, but she hardly noticed. She was numb to the cold water that seeped through her jeans.

The detective stood in silence beside her with his arms folded, making her feel like a prisoner at her own house. She closed her eyes and pictured John's victims. All eleven of them. *She was married to a monster.* She sipped her water, trying to ease the ache in her stomach. She wondered if the police would find evidence of more killings…under her own roof. It seemed unfathomable.

John could be distant at times, absorbed in his work. But she'd assumed it was his dedication to justice. She wondered how many nights she thought he was working late in the city when he was really strangling female high school teachers he'd been stalking for weeks.

Two investigators crossed the lawn and entered the oversized garden shed Cameron and John had built to match the house. Cameron had always admired the quaint charm of the miniature white structure with blue trim. Until she watched an investigator emerge carrying evidence bags filled with rope and pruning shears. The second investigator followed, holding a shovel in her gloved hand.

Cameron's breath caught at the sight of the evidence bags. Anxiety rose in her chest in a way she hadn't felt in years. She took a gulp from her water, trying to flush the feeling away.

Her eyes followed the investigators until they were back inside the house. She stared at the garden shed again. It reminded her of the shed at her previous home, which lacked the magazine-cover charm of this one. Where she'd spent two miserable years of her life. Before she'd met John, and he'd made her feel alive again.

All these years being married to John, she thought she'd been the one with a secret.

CHAPTER FOUR

"Are you sure there isn't anyone I can call for you?"

Cameron looked away from Detective Mulholland's sharp blue eyes as he stood in her front doorway. It was late afternoon by the time they finished searching her home, and the sky had resolved to a dark slate. She was glad to see the Parkers had at some point retreated inside their home to, hopefully, mind their own business.

"No. Thank you."

He wore a look of concern when her eyes turned back to his.

"I'll call a friend," she lied.

"I'm very sorry for what you've been through."

Cameron fought the tears back. She just needed him to go.

"If you think of anything else, let me know." He pulled out his phone, gave it a quick scan. "I'm planning to meet a CSI team at your Cle Elum cabin tomorrow to search the premises. So long as Snoqualmie Pass reopens."

He handed her his card. Her fingers brushed his when she accepted it.

"And, you should know we are having a press conference tonight to announce we are charging your late husband with the murders of eleven women. I appreciate you bringing those photos in today. That was brave."

Cameron nodded, unable to speak, and closed the door behind him. She looked around her empty house. Several cabinet doors had been left ajar. Framed photos hung at an angle from the walls.

She let the tears spill from her overflowing eyes as she marched to the kitchen, hardly noticing her normally artfully arranged throw pillows in a messy heap on her living room sofa. She started to heat hot water for tea but thought better of it. She went straight for John's liquor cabinet in the adjacent dining room. She hardly ever drank anything stronger than wine.

Cameron pulled a half-full bottle of whiskey out from the cabinet and poured herself a generous three fingers. She took a drink before climbing her curved staircase. She looked down at her beloved leopard-print stair runner, which was no comfort to her today.

When she reached the landing in the middle of the staircase, she paused to look at the abstract modern painting John had bought for her. She'd fallen in love with the piece when she first saw it in a gallery in Chelsea when she and John had taken a trip to New York a few years back. He surprised her by buying it for her and having it shipped to their home, even though it cost more than his Porsche.

She loved the painting because no matter how many times she looked at it, she could always see something new. Now, all she saw as she looked at the paint running down the side of the canvas was dripping blood. She stared at the swirl of bright colors and envisioned a woman screaming as John strangled the life from her.

She gripped the wrought iron banister and pulled herself to the top of the stairs. When she entered the master bedroom, she took another drink and grimaced as the whiskey burned the back of her throat. She had made her California King before leaving for the cabin, but thanks to the CSI team, it was now a disarray of blankets and sheets atop her bare mattress. All her clothes had been removed from her walk-in closet and were piled high on top of her bedding.

How many times had she made love to a serial killer in that bed? She didn't ask Detective Mulholland for any details of John's crimes. But she'd read about the Teacher Killer's murders in the news and had seen enough from John's photos to know that all the women had been raped before he killed them. How many times had he come home in the late hours of the night after raping and strangling someone and pressed his naked body against hers as he kissed her good night?

She turned away from her bed and saw her underwear drawer was ajar. She yanked it open and saw her normally organized bras and panties were a jumbled mess. She closed the drawer, slowly, shaking her head. She rubbed her arms and scanned her room, feeling a chill despite the warm house.

She forced down the last finger of whiskey and placed a hand over her mouth when it threatened to come back up.

These last three months she'd mourned for John, and for herself. She'd also pitied him that his life was cut short. Now, she realized he'd gotten the easy way out. And she was the only one left to live with what he'd done.

She supported herself against the dresser and willed herself not to throw up. Movement outside her bedroom window caught her eye. She crept forward and drew aside the curtain.

In the place of the police vehicles, two vans had pulled up to the curb in front of her house. She recognized the signs on each of them as belonging to the two biggest local news stations. As reporters and camera crews jumped out of the vans, Cameron spotted the Parkers emerging from their house onto their front lawn.

Cameron backed away from the window and pulled the silk curtains closed. John had always despised their neighbors across the street with their matching electric cars and lingering looks. He had complained about how much time they spent in their front yard, feeding off everyone else's business.

They had never bothered Cameron. She'd always thought them friendly, even if they had too much time on their hands. Now she was starting to see what John meant. And he had much more to hide than Cameron.

She stood still in her darkened room and tried to keep from hyperventilating. When Detective Mulholland said they were doing a press conference early that evening, Cameron thought she'd have more time to prepare herself. Not that another hour could've readied her for the world learning that John was a serial killer. It hadn't occurred to her that the media would show up at her home. *Was there no such thing as privacy these days?*

Her phone rang in her sweatshirt pocket. When she pulled it out, she didn't recognize the number.

"Hello?"

"Mrs. Prescott, this is Ashlynn Hendricks from the *Elliot Bay Tribune*. I wanted to ask if you ever suspected your husband was the Teacher—"

Cameron ended the call with a shaking hand, not even bothering to ask how the reporter had gotten her number. Seconds later, her phone rang again. It was a call from the same number. Cameron rejected the call and powered off her phone before throwing it onto her unmade bed as if it were a venomous snake.

Her doorbell startled her, the charming chime no longer charming. Cameron spun and ran down the stairs, fueled with a burst of anger. *How dare they come onto my property?*

In a few quick strides she positioned herself at the front door. She squinted through the peephole to find a blonde woman in a blue blazer holding a microphone in her hand. A man holding a video camera stood a few feet behind her.

"Get off my property!" Cameron screamed through the closed door.

The woman didn't even flinch before responding. "We just have a few questions if you could—"

"Leave or I'll call the police!" Cameron shouted even louder than she had the first time.

She watched the reporter roll her eyes in disgust. "Fine." She turned and waved to the man behind her. "Let's go."

Cameron sank against the door, her rage shifting from the reporters to John. Her eyes settled on the framed black-and-white wedding photo of her and John, perched atop her entryway table. How could he do this to her? To those women?

She grabbed the frame and hurled the picture across the room, sending it crashing through her living room window. Seconds later, a spotlight shone against the broken window.

Cameron let out a cry of frustration as the news crew captured her moment of rage for the world to see.

CHAPTER FIVE

Cameron woke to a relentless knocking on her front door. Light filtered into the room through the closed curtains of her guest room. She sat up and looked at the bedside clock. *7:15*. She remembered taking one of the sleeping pills she'd been prescribed after John's death. At least she had finally drifted off in the early hours of the morning.

The knocking continued. She threw back her comforter and moved to the window of the guest room. She didn't have the energy to deal with reporters again.

A local news van pulled away from the curb in front of her house when she pushed the silk fabric aside. She recognized the champagne-colored Bentley that was parked in front of the van. Relief flooded through her as she trod downstairs.

She checked the peephole before opening the door wide.

"Simon," she managed to say as his muscular arms enveloped her in an embrace.

"I told that news crew that, as your attorney, I'd be suing them for harassment and emotional damages if they didn't leave. Although, they know they're within their rights—unless they step foot on your property—so I'm guessing they'll be back. Why didn't you answer my calls?" Simon stepped back, keeping his hands on her shoulders. "I saw the press conference last night. I've been worried about you."

He dropped his hands, and Cameron stepped aside for him to come in.

"I'm sorry. I turned my phone off last night."

She caught her reflection in the round mirror on her entryway wall, startled to discover she never washed off her makeup last night. Her mascara was smudged around her eyes like a raccoon and her blonde curls were a matted mess around her face. But, in that moment, she was beyond caring.

Simon followed her into the living room. "Are you all right?"

"I've been better."

"Who did that? The press?" He pointed to the piece of cardboard she had duct-taped over the broken window.

"No, of course not. I did it. I was upset."

"I'm as shocked as you. Well, maybe not quite, but I'm shocked." He took a seat on her pink velvet couch.

Cameron sank into a zebra-print armchair across from him. Despite the early hour, Simon wore a designer bespoke suit. His tan looked unnatural for the middle of a Seattle winter. He was only a few years older than John, but his hair had been white for the entire ten years Cameron had known him as John's partner.

"How can the police be so sure?" Simon crossed one leg over the other, exposing his bare ankle above his Italian leather loafers. "They're under a lot of pressure to soothe the public hysteria surrounding The Teacher Killer. Seems like an easy way for the cops to pin a ton of unsolved cases on a defenseless dead man."

Cameron flinched at the word *dead*, but it didn't stop Simon from continuing.

"This makes them look great, while John never gets the right to a trial. Not to mention, the reputation of our law firm. My standing in the legal community might never recover from these false accusations. What did the police tell you? They can't have DNA evidence for all eleven of the murders they're charging him with?"

Finally, he paused long enough for her to get a word in.

"They found his DNA under the fingernails of the West Seattle teacher killed last summer. And at the scene of a murder nearly thirty years ago. She was John's substitute English teacher. The police believe she was his first."

"Maybe there's another explanation for his DNA at that old crime scene. I can have my investigator look into it. The police do get things wrong, you know." Simon leaned forward. "And those photos! How do they know—"

Cameron threw both hands in the air. "He did it! Okay? Just stop! *I* was the one who found those photos, not the police. Trust me, there is no other *explanation*."

Simon tilted his face back to maintain eye contact, and Cameron realized she'd stood from her chair.

"John wasn't who either of us thought he was. He was a sick, psychopathic monster!"

Simon stared at her as if she'd slapped him. He'd never seen her even raise her voice and she had yelled loudly enough for the Parkers to hear.

"Simon, I can't do this. I know you're trying to help. But I saw the photos, and it was him. And the police have even more evidence. They'd been building a case against John for months before he died. Suspecting him for longer."

Simon opened his mouth in rebuttal, but Cameron spoke first. "Please, don't." She shook her head.

Simon looked away, but not before she registered the pain in his eyes.

He stared out her front window. "I just can't believe it. We'd been friends for twenty years."

"I know." Cameron exhaled. "But it's true."

An uncomfortable silence filled the room until Cameron spoke again. "Look, I appreciate you coming, but I have to get ready for work."

He looked up at her blankly.

"I have patients. Appointments."

Although she had yet to think of how she would face them. But she couldn't hide in her house forever with reporters parked outside her home, making her a prisoner.

She already took time off after John went missing. She was losing money on payroll and her office lease as it was. She couldn't afford to *not* see patients.

"I understand." Simon's voice was soft. "But I wish you'd come to me before going to the police. You need someone with you who knows how to protect your rights. I want to be present if the police want to speak with you again. As your attorney and your friend." He put his hands on his thighs and stood from her couch. "And if you need anything, and I mean *anything,* you call me. If those reporters come back, let me know. I know how to handle them."

"Okay." Cameron managed a weak smile before she followed him to the door.

He turned when they reached the entryway. "Have the police said anything about searching your home? Or the cabin?"

Cameron nodded. "They searched everything here for hours yesterday. They couldn't get to the cabin because of the storm, but they're heading there this morning. As long as the pass is open now."

Simon's eyes widened. "*What!* Why didn't you call me? Did they show you a warrant?"

"I—I didn't ask. With the evidence they have against John, I assumed they had one. They said there might be more victims. And Simon, at this point I'm not going to stand in the way of them finding out."

"They're searching your cabin today?"

"That's what the detective told me."

"I'm going up there. I want to make sure they aren't planting evidence. Who is this detective, anyway?"

"Simon, I know you want to help but—"

He placed his hands on her shoulders. "Look, John may be dead. But *you* still have to live with the consequences of whatever they find. Or plant."

John shared the same mistrust of the police that Simon did, and it was something that Cameron never understood.

37

She always chalked it up to him being a jaded defense attorney. But she was too exhausted to argue with Simon.

"Do you want to come with me?"

"No. But thank you, Simon. I appreciate you going."

"Oh, here." He pulled two envelopes from his suit jacket pocket. "We still get some occasional mail for John sent to the firm."

She took the envelopes from his outstretched hand. One looked to be from a bank. "Thanks."

Simon dropped his gaze to the letters. "I mean it. If you need help—with anything—I want you to come to me." His attorney eyes searched hers. "You going to be okay?"

"Yeah, I'll be fine."

They both knew it was a lie, but he didn't argue before going out the door.

CHAPTER SIX

"Bag up all the bedding and everything from the closet." Detective Tanner Mulholland stood in the doorway to the bedroom at the Cle Elum cabin and watched the CSI team strip the comforter off the queen-size bed.

Their luminol spray hadn't picked up any traces of blood in the cabin other than the kitchen sink. Since John Prescott used this as a hunting cabin, they would have to test it to find out if it was animal or human. This didn't surprise Tanner. Aside from the superficial postmortem markings Prescott made on his victims' backs, they were killed without any blood spill.

He thought about Prescott's widow, Cameron. How she must've felt coming up here and then learning she'd slept in the same bed where her husband had tortured, raped, and murdered a young woman. Maybe more than one.

Her shock at her husband's crimes seemed genuine. But it didn't explain why she refused to hold his gaze for more than a few seconds. She could be ashamed for having married a serial killer, but his gut told him it was more than that.

Tanner turned from the doorway as the team continued to bag the potential evidence and walked out the front door. Other than the traces of blood in the kitchen sink, their search so far of the cabin hadn't yielded anything. His breath escaped his mouth in a cloud of white when he stepped out into the frigid mountain air. Snow crunched beneath his boots as he moved through the surrounding wooded area toward the cadaver dogs and their handlers.

Tanner had instantly recognized the deceased woman John photographed in his cabin when Cameron had brought the photos to the homicide unit. He'd suspected Alicia Lopez had been one of the Teacher Killer's victims, but until seeing the photos he hadn't been sure. He'd refrained from telling Prescott's widow the entire implications of her discovery. While Alicia was the only woman photographed at the cabin in the photos Cameron found, Tanner suspected she wasn't the only woman Prescott killed up here.

Alicia was one of two Seattle teachers who went missing the summer before last, only hours apart. Alicia went missing first, never returning home to her family after an evening jog at Discovery Park. Olivia Rossi, a twenty-eight-year-old Ballard High School teacher went missing hours later after leaving a Queen Anne yoga studio where she taught a late-night class. When her boyfriend reported her missing the next morning, her car was still parked at the yoga studio.

Before seeing the photos, there were two things that made Tanner reluctant to attribute their disappearances to the Teacher Killer. First, all the rest of Prescott's victims had lived alone and were found murdered in their own beds.

Second, Prescott was flying home from California when both women went missing. He landed at SeaTac airport at midnight, two hours after Olivia was captured on video leaving the yoga studio.

The cadaver dogs and their handlers disappeared behind a thick patch of trees. Tanner started treading through the snow in their direction when he heard tires move atop the cabin's packed snow drive. Tanner turned to see a two-door Bentley with chains on its tires skid to a stop behind his Dodge Ram. Due to the snow on the pass, Tanner had opted to drive his own truck instead of his department-issued Ford Fusion.

He half-expected to see Cameron get out of the car. Tanner didn't bother to hide his disdain when he recognized the white-haired man in a pinstripe suit who climbed out of the coupe. He was the only defense attorney Tanner disliked as much as Prescott. Or, almost as much.

"We're in the middle of searching this property, Simon. You need to get back in your car. If you even have a right to be here," Tanner called out. "This is private property."

Simon wasted no time in marching straight toward the detective, his loafers disappearing into the snow with each step. He scoffed before pointing at his own chest. "*I* am here on behalf of my client, Cameron Prescott, to make sure that *you* are staying within your rights. I sure hope you have a warrant to be tearing this place apart, Detective Mulholland."

Tanner smiled and pulled a folded white paper from his coat pocket. "I do."

The sharp bark from a cadaver dog echoed through the woods. Tanner turned but kept an eye on Simon.

"Mulholland!" a K-9 handler called out. "We've got something!"

Tanner started through the snow when he heard Simon following closely behind.

He stopped and pointed to Simon's Bentley. "Get back in your car! Or I'll cuff you and put you in the back of mine."

"Fine. But I'm not leaving."

Tanner watched Simon retreat before he ran toward the thick patch of trees.

CHAPTER SEVEN

Cameron looked up at the two-story office building from the front seat of her Lexus. After Simon left, she had showered and put on just enough makeup to look presentable. Her practice was on the top floor, and she saw the graffiti even before she turned into the parking lot. Even from the street, there was no mistaking what the freshly spray-painted letters covering the entire front wall of her practice spelled out.

KILLER had been inscribed big enough to make the message clear to passing traffic. The parking lot was unusually empty for a Monday morning. Cameron worried that the vandal's tag had scared away some of her patients.

She climbed out of her car and ascended the steps to her practice. The only cars she recognized in the parking lot were those belonging to her front office manager and dental assistant. Her hygienist and other dental assistant must be running late.

Erin and Daniela lifted their heads from behind the front desk when Cameron came through the door. The lobby was empty.

Her office manager's expression turned awkward when their eyes met. *This is even worse than after John died. What would people say now?* Cameron wondered. *I'm sorry your husband turned out to be a heinous serial killer?*

"Um," Daniela started. "I—I saw the news last night. I'm so sorry."

"Me too," Cameron said. *What else was there to say?*

She regretted not taking the day off, even though she couldn't afford it. She moved behind the desk toward her office. "We need to call the police about that graffiti." Cameron tried to sound casual, as if it weren't personal. *And her fault.*

"I already did," Daniela said. "They said they would send someone out when they could, but it probably wouldn't be today. They're short staffed due to budget cuts. If we want something done sooner, they said we could go into our local precinct and file a report."

Cameron exhaled in the doorway to her office. She wasn't going into another police station today. "That'll take too long. I want it removed. Skip the police report and call someone to come out and get it off the building, please."

"But don't you—"

"No." Cameron's voice came out sharper than she intended. "Thank you," she added.

"Also," Erin said before Cameron could disappear into her office. "Liv and Maria called out sick."

Cameron turned to her dental assistant. "When?"

"Earlier this morning."

"And there were ten voicemails when I got here." Daniela gave her a wary look. "All but one of today's patients have canceled their appointments. So, all you have is a filling at noon. Should I see if they can reschedule?"

"No." Cameron hoped the firmness in her tone might help her gain some control. "I'll see the patient at noon. In the meantime, call around and see if we can get that graffiti removed—today. And confirm tomorrow's appointments. While you're at it, check if any of them might want to come in today. Other than cleanings, I guess, since Maria is out sick."

Her employees glanced at each other before Daniela answered. "Okay."

"If you need me, I'll be in my office." Cameron slammed the door shut behind her.

Cameron checked the time in the corner of her computer screen. Her noon appointment didn't show, and it was now almost two. She spent the entire morning thinking about John while she listened to the blast of the pressure washer against the exterior wall of her office, stuck in a cloud of anger she couldn't find her way out of.

She racked her brain for signs that John was a murderer, but there was nothing. They'd been happy. He brightened her world when he came into her life, filled it with laughter and love. It was unfathomable that she could've shared her life with him for so long and not known who he really was.

Although, she hadn't been completely honest with him either. Had they both kept a safe emotional distance, only allowing the other to see what they wanted them to?

She scrolled down her laptop screen and tried to focus on the list of real estate agents that came up when she searched *best Seattle realtors*. A light knock on her office door interrupted her thoughts before it swung open, and her dental assistant appeared.

"Could I come in?" Erin held a paper in her hand.

Cameron closed her laptop and leaned back in her chair. "Of course." Erin was probably wondering when she and Daniela could go home, since their only patient of the day was a no-show.

Erin marched toward Cameron's desk with an outstretched arm. "This is my letter of resignation," she said, before Cameron could reach for the paper.

Cameron knew she shouldn't be surprised. *Who would want to work for the wife of a notorious serial killer?* But it still stung. She had hoped for a little more loyalty from her staff.

Cameron took the paper and set it on her desk. She folded her hands before looking up at the young assistant. *Keep it professional,* she reminded herself. "We'll be sorry to see you go."

Her assistant nodded. "Thank you. Is there anything else you'd like me to do today?"

Cameron forced a polite smile. "No, thanks. You can go."

Erin lingered for a moment, as if debating something she wanted to say, before she left Cameron's office. Cameron glared at the resignation letter, her vision blurring from tears when she read the first line.

Please accept this letter of resignation from—

She used both hands to crumble the letter into a tiny ball. It was the size of a golf ball when she noticed Daniela standing inside her doorway. Cameron tossed the paper into the wastebasket. The wad of paper landed beside the framed photo of her and John that she'd dumped in the trash first thing that morning.

"Maria called out sick again for tomorrow, so I canceled her cleaning appointments."

She was grateful that Daniela didn't mention the tears Cameron was now wiping from her eyes. Her office manager hesitated. Unlike Erin, Daniela had worked for her for nearly ten years. She was more than an employee to Cameron.

"We've had more patients call to cancel this week. Most said they were switching dentists." Daniela bit her lip while she waited for Cameron's response.

Cameron leaned forward and rested her elbows on her desk. "All right. Let's cancel any remaining appointments and close for the week. And, before you go, can you post a job opening for a full-time dental assistant? You can use the same listing we posted last time."

"Sure." Daniela didn't look surprised. She grabbed the door handle. "Oh, and the graffiti's gone."

"Good."

"Can I get you anything before I go?"

"No. Thank you, Daniela."

She closed the door softly behind her, leaving Cameron alone in her office.

Cameron opened her laptop and forced her attention back to her realtor search. She couldn't live in that house anymore. Especially not when she was surrounded by neighbors who would smile to her face and gossip behind her back for the rest of her life.

According to an online estimator, her home was worth nearly three and a half million. She was into it for over two, with the extensive remodel they'd done right after they were married. After selling costs, she'd still have enough to start over, but it wasn't about the money. She needed to be free of the home, and John's shadow lurking over her. It might not be possible. But she was going to try.

Cameron wasn't sure how long she'd been staring at the screen when she heard the front office door open and shut. She glanced at the time and saw it was after three. Daniela must've finally gone home.

Cameron rubbed her eyes and shut down her computer. She'd continue her realtor search at home over a drink. When she reached for the Burberry coat John bought her last year for Christmas, she spotted the white envelopes Simon had dropped off that morning protruding from the side pocket.

She pulled them out and used the letter opener on her desk to open John's mail. After tossing aside John's license renewal letter from the Washington State Bar Association, she slid the paper out of the second envelope. It was from a bank she'd never heard of.

She reread the statement several times. It couldn't be right. How could she have a second mortgage on her home without knowing? She looked to the top of the bill. Only one name on the statement: *John Prescott.*

Two months before his death, John closed a cash-out refinance loan on their Laurelhurst home for one million dollars. The words on the page blurred the longer she stared at the mortgage statement. She let the paper fall from her hand onto her desk.

"Son of a bitch."

CHAPTER EIGHT

Cameron stood in her kitchen and poured herself a second glass of Syrah, spilling a large drop onto the mortgage statement atop her marble counter. She used her fingers to brush the wine off the paper, smearing it across the twelve-thousand-dollar payment that had been due the first of the month.

It didn't make sense. They'd always had money. *Did he know the police were coming for him?* It didn't seem like it from what Detective Mulholland had told her. According to him, the evidence against John was mostly circumstantial—until recently.

She opened her banking app on her phone and checked the joint account she'd shared with John. She took a large drink from her wine after seeing the balance. With the added mortgage payment, she only had enough to cover her expenses for another month or so without any income from her dental practice.

What had John done with the million-dollar loan?

The doorbell chimed. Cameron jumped, nearly dropping her phone. Taking a breath, she remembered the appointment she had set up with the realtor she spoke with when she got home from work. She checked her front door camera app, recognizing the red-haired real estate agent from the photo on her website. The agent beamed a full-lipped, bleached-teeth smile when Cameron opened the door.

"Hi, I'm Shay." She thrust her open palm toward Cameron.

She returned Shay's strong handshake. "I'm Cameron. Thanks for coming so soon."

"Well, it was perfect timing when you called. I was at an open house just up the street. Should I take off my shoes?" Shay pointed at her red-soled stilettos after stepping inside.

"No, that's okay. I'll show you around."

The realtor followed Cameron through the living room, her heels clacking atop the hardwood floor. "I love the modern-eclectic theme you have going on here. Very glam."

"Thanks." Cameron led her past the white baby grand toward the kitchen.

"Can I ask why you're selling?"

"It's just too much house for me to maintain."

"I get it. How many square feet again?"

Cameron turned when they reached the kitchen. "Forty-two hundred."

"These look like recent renovations." Shay ran her hand atop the marble countertop.

Cameron nodded. "I did a full renovation eight years ago."

"And you live here alone?" The realtor asked, as they moved into the dining room.

"I do now. My husband passed away a few months ago."

Shay put a hand over her heart. "Oh, I'm so sorry."

Well, turns out he was a serial killer so it's probably for the best. Cameron forced a slight smile before leading her around the rest of the main level. "Thank you."

When they reached the staircase, Cameron placed her hand on the banister. "Ready to see the upstairs?"

She turned when Shay didn't respond. The realtor gaped at the enlarged photo that hung high on the wall beneath the vaulted ceiling. Cameron would need a ladder to reach it, and it was one of the few of John that she had yet to take down.

She remembered the day the photo was taken like it was yesterday. She and John had just gotten their private pilot's licenses. He had his arm around her, and they stood in front of their newly purchased Cessna. They both wore huge grins, and Cameron proudly held up the keys to their new plane.

"Is that your husband?" Shay still stared at the photo.

"My late husband, yes."

Shay turned to meet Cameron's gaze. "What was his name?"

Cameron gripped the railing. She could see from the realtor's expression that she already knew. Cameron figured there was no point in trying to hide it. It had been all over the news. "John. John Prescott."

"The Teacher Killer?"

Cameron nodded, holding Shay's eyes, fighting the shame.

"No wonder you want you to sell." Shay took a deep breath and appeared to compose herself. "I probably don't have to tell you this, but that's going to affect your selling price." The pleasant professionalism had returned to her voice.

"I'm sorry," she added, reading the disappointment on Cameron's face.

Shay eyed the staircase with caution instead of the awe Cameron saw on her face when she first walked in. "Let's see the upstairs."

They finished the home tour in silence.

"So, given your circumstances," Shay said, when they returned downstairs.

My circumstances, Cameron thought. *What a nice way of saying I was married to a serial killer.*

"I wouldn't expect you to get more than two point five to two point seven."

Cameron felt her jaw drop. "I was hoping for three point five."

Shay folded her arms across her chest. "The problem is, when people find out this was the home of a serial killer, most buyers will lose interest. We could start by listing it a little higher, say two point nine. But you should be aware that offers will likely come in much lower. And at some point, you might have to decide how long you're willing to stay here."

Cameron sank to the bottom stair and rested her elbows on her knees. After selling costs and John's second mortgage, she would owe a few hundred thousand if she sold the house for less than three million—which she couldn't afford. But if her dental practice went under, she couldn't afford to stay here either. And she couldn't live in this house much longer before the memories drove her insane.

"Fine. How about two point nine-nine?"

"Great. I'll draw up a contract and bring it by tomorrow. Will this same time be okay?"

Anytime is okay since I won't be seeing patients at my office. The thought of spending the week alone in this house, surrounded by reminders of her life with John filled her stomach with dread. She could go to a hotel, but she'd only run out of money sooner. "Yes, this same time is fine."

"Oh, don't get up." Shay raised her palms in the air. "I can let myself out."

"Thank you," Cameron managed to say.

"No problem. I'll see you tomorrow."

After the door closed, Cameron buried her face in her hands. *I'm going to be known for the rest of my life as that woman who was married to the Teacher Killer.* Even though he'd been mauled to death by a couple of bears, it still seemed like John got the easier way out.

John was a charismatic and persuasive man. Unlike her first husband, John had made her feel safe. He never even raised his voice at her. She wondered now if that was because he was detached from human emotion, when she thought it meant he loved her. He seemed like her knight in shining armor after being married to Miles.

Remembering John's life insurance policy, she jumped to her feet. She knew he had one—at John's insistence, they both took out policies before they were married. She'd been forced to wait to claim the policy until John was officially declared dead by the Seattle Medical Examiner's Office, which had taken until last month. But thinking her dental practice would pay the bills, she hadn't gotten around to claiming it yet.

She climbed the stairs and entered John's office. After flicking on the light, she found his file cabinet drawers pulled out, and their contents left in a messy stack on the desk. A few of the files had fallen onto the floor.

Thanks to John's meticulous organization, it took her less than a minute to find the file labeled *Life Insurance,* even in the state they'd been left by the CSI team. She thumbed through the statements. At first, all she could find were the statements from her own policy.

At the back of the file, she found the statements from John's policy. But there were only a handful, with the most recent statement dated two years ago. She took the most recent one downstairs to the kitchen where she had left her phone.

She called the insurance company and keyed in John's policy number. After being placed on hold, she finished her glass of Syrah. She debated pouring herself another glass when a female voice came over her phone's speaker.

"Hello, thank you for waiting. How can I help you today?"

"Hi. Yes, I'm calling about my late husband's life insurance policy. He passed away, and I need to file a claim."

"I'm so sorry to hear that, ma'am."

"Thank you."

"Could I have the policy holder's full name, date of birth, and social security number?"

"John Graham Prescott. July 12, 1976." She read John's social security number off the top of the page.

"And with whom am I speaking?"

"Cameron Prescott."

She heard the clatter of keystrokes on the other end of the call.

"I just need you to answer a security question that was created by the policy holder. What's your favorite animal?"

John didn't have a favorite animal—unless he was hunting them. He was allergic to dogs and repulsed by cats. "Um. I'm not sure. Is there another security question I can answer?"

"I'm sorry, ma'am, but no. Our system requires this answer before I can move to the next screen."

Cameron pinched the bridge of her nose with her thumb and forefinger. "I don't know. Bear?" It was the first thing that popped into her head, and she immediately regretted it. But the woman spoke before she could take it back.

"Thanks for that. Just a moment while I pull up the policy."

You've got to be kidding me. The woman's keystrokes filled the void while Cameron waited.

"So, it looks like the only policy we have on file for John is that same policy number you typed in. And the policy was cashed out and closed two years ago."

"What?"

"I'm sorry, ma'am?"

"Wait. *All of it?* It was a million-dollar policy."

"Well, no. You can only withdraw the cash value you've put into the policy. So, it looks like the policy was cashed out for $49,823."

"That doesn't make any sense. There must be some mistake. He wouldn't have." John was so adamant about them having insurance coverage. On everything. "I mean, why would he cash out a million-dollar policy for fifty grand?"

"Unfortunately, I'm not able to answer that. There are a variety of reasons why people cash out their policies: financial hardship or—"

"Right, of course. Thank you." Cameron pressed *End Call* on her screen.

John didn't need that money for *their* life. *So, what did he use it for?*

CHAPTER NINE

It was dark when Tanner turned west onto I-90 back to Seattle. The two female remains that the cadaver dogs had discovered on Prescott's property were on their way to the Seattle Medical Examiner's Office. Both bodies looked to be at the same stage of decomposition.

Wet snow fell against his windshield and Tanner turned on his wipers. It would be tomorrow before the medical examiner compared the dental records of the two bodies to the teachers who went missing the summer before last. But Tanner was positive they would match.

With the help of a local contractor and his backhoe, along with an anthropologist from Seattle's Medical Examiner Office, it took the forensic team most of the day to remove the bodies from the frozen soil while being careful not to disturb any potential evidence. Movement out his side window caught Tanner's eye. He turned to see Simon Castelli's Bentley speed past him in the adjacent lane, going way too fast for the snowy road conditions. Tanner watched the Bentley's headlights disappear around a bend up ahead as he imagined finding the luxury car upside down in a snow-filled ditch on the side of the mountain pass.

What a pain in the ass. After the K-9s discovered the bodies, Tanner assigned an officer to babysit Simon to ensure he didn't disturb the scene.

Tanner stepped on the gas to get around a slow-moving semitruck. It was too dark to see the sheer mountain peaks that lined both sides of the winding Interstate, and Tanner kept his eyes on the snowy road ahead while he chewed his gum and thought about what they'd uncovered.

Although the two bodies buried at Prescott's cabin confirmed Tanner's suspicions that the two Seattle teachers who went missing were victims of The Teacher Killer, it also presented a problem.

Every summer for the last decade, a Seattle teacher who lived alone was raped and strangled in her home. With the exception of the summer these two teachers went missing. So, *why two? And why not choose women who lived alone like all the rest? Why stray from his MO?*

But what bothered Tanner most of all is that John couldn't have taken these women. Killed them, yes. But he was boarding a flight in California at the time they went missing. Which meant he had help.

After he finished searching the Prescotts' Laurelhurst home yesterday, Tanner searched the traffic cameras on I-90 between Issaquah and the Cle Elum exit to John's cabin on the night the teachers went missing. He'd been surprised at what he found.

In the distance, Tanner spotted Castelli's brakes light up as the Bentley wound through the foothills of the mountain. Tanner's truck closed in on the coupe, and he chided himself for the dissatisfaction that he felt seeing Simon's car unscathed and still on the road.

He wondered if the defense attorney had already called Prescott's widow and told her what they'd found at the cabin. Tanner wanted to see the look on her face when he delivered the news but knew that Castelli would likely beat him to the punch. Nevertheless, Tanner lifted his phone, found the number Cameron gave him yesterday, and placed the call through his blue tooth.

Ringing echoed through his truck speakers. She answered after the second ring.

"Hello?"

He recognized the fatigue in her voice.

"Hi, Cameron. This is Detective Mulholland. I'm driving back from your cabin. I was hoping I could speak with you this evening about what we found."

"Okay. What is it?"

So, Simon hadn't already told her. Or he had, but she wanted to hear his version. "I'd rather speak with you in person, if that's all right."

Mulholland kept an eye on the Bentley.

"Oh. Of course. There's actually something I'd like to ask you too. About John."

"Sure. Would you be able to come down to the Homicide Unit where we spoke this weekend?"

"Yes, what time?"

Tanner checked the clock on his dash. "How about eight, or eight-thirty?"

"Eight is fine. See you then."

Tanner ended the call and stared through the falling snow at Castelli's taillights up ahead. Cameron Prescott was a smart woman. A dentist. *She had to know something.* Although, Tanner had witnessed Prescott's compelling ability to convince a jury of a guilty man's innocence in the courtroom more than once. Tanner doubted anyone, other than the victims, had seen his true self. But that didn't explain what Tanner saw on the traffic camera footage.

CHAPTER TEN

"*Two* bodies?"

Cameron wasn't sure why her voice sounded so shocked. She had already seen the graphic photos John took after killing a woman in the same bed she shared with him at the cabin. The level of John's betrayal—his derangement—didn't seem to change whether he killed one or one hundred.

Detective Mulholland nodded. "It will be tomorrow before the medical examiner is able to ID them, but I believe they were both teachers who went missing the summer before last."

Cameron remembered their disappearances making the news. There was speculation that they were taken by the Teacher Killer. *By John.* But, since the rest of the Teacher Killer's victims were killed and found in their own homes, other theories prevailed.

The door to the interview room flew open.

"Why are you talking to her in here?" Simon stood in the doorway, briefcase in hand, the irritation obvious in his tone.

He gestured to the one-way mirror that served as a wall beyond the detective and Cameron. "She's not a suspect."

Cameron noticed his loafers were wet, along with the lower part of his suit pants.

The detective offered Simon a relaxed smile. "Well *hello* to you, too, Mr. Castelli. Cameron agreed to speak in here and be recorded in case she recalls anything that might help us."

"I don't see how that requires her to be questioned in a police interview room." Simon stepped inside the room. He let out an exacerbated sigh when he plopped into the chair beside Cameron. "Why didn't you answer my calls?" His voice held the same irritation as it had when he spoke to Mulholland. "I told you not to speak to him without me. I can't help you if you don't take my advice."

Simon ran a hand through his usually carefully styled hair, which was as disheveled as Cameron had ever seen it.

"I'm sorry. I appreciate you trying to protect me—I do. After Detective Mulholland called, I turned my phone off. I keep getting calls from reporters. I don't know how they're getting my number. I need to get a new one."

"That's all right, Cam." Simon's voice softened as he straightened his suit jacket. "Changing your number is a good idea."

Simon turned his attention to the detective.

"I was just informing Cameron of what we found at her cabin today." Mulholland locked his sharp blue eyes with Cameron's. "I know you've been through quite a shock these last few days. But there are some questions surrounding how your husband got these women to your cabin—assuming they're the two teachers I think they are. I'm not sure if you recall, but John was flying back from California when both of these women went missing. His flight landed at SeaTac about two hours after Olivia Rossi was last seen leaving a Queen Anne yoga studio, which was three hours after Alicia Lopez—the woman in John's photographs—was last seen alive."

He paused to search Cameron's eyes.

What is he saying? "John traveled for work periodically. I'm sorry—I'm not sure what you're asking me?"

Simon held up his palm for Cameron to be quiet and turned to Mulholland. "This is all speculation. You haven't even ID'd the bodies yet."

"I think John had an accomplice," Mulholland continued. "Not for all his killings, but for the two women whose bodies we found at your cabin."

John's cabin. But she didn't correct him. "An accomplice?"

"Or maybe John was framed," Simon interjected. "How could John kidnap women and take them to his cabin while he's in California? He couldn't be in two places at once. It's called reasonable doubt, detective."

Cameron placed a hand on Simon's arm. "He wasn't framed. He was *in* the photos with the dead woman. He was *there* with her. He killed her." Cameron swallowed as the image of John standing shirtless, admiring the naked dead woman in their cabin's bedroom flooded her mind. "And he looked like he was enjoying it."

"My best guess is that John's accomplice was a client of his," Mulholland said. "Someone John could've paid to kidnap the women and bring them to his cabin. Were there any clients he stayed in contact with?"

Cameron shook her head. "Not that I know of."

The detective looked to Simon. "Can you think of anyone John represented who might've been willing to do something like this?"

Cameron turned to see Simon's reaction. He seemed pensive for a few moments before he answered. "No."

Mulholland's gaze returned to Cameron as he withdrew a stick of gum from his pocket. Without taking his eyes off hers, he unwrapped it and folded the gum into his mouth.

"And where were you on the evenings of June 19 and 20 of 2020?"

"I—" Cameron's voice faltered. Was he asking her for an *alibi*? "I don't—"

"You don't have to answer that, Cameron," Simon said. "I don't see the relevance of my client's whereabouts, Detective. That's ridiculous. Like she'd even remember that far back, anyway."

"The reason I'm asking," Mulholland responded, his eyes staying fixed on Cameron's, "is because I found your Lexus on a traffic camera on I-90 heading east about two miles before the exit to your Cle Elum cabin on the evening of June 19. The same night both women went missing when John was flying back from California."

"I—I wasn't…." Cameron shot a dumbfounded look at Simon.

"Don't say anything, Cameron." Simon held out his hand in front of her and turned to confront Mulholland. "Driving on an interstate doesn't make Cameron guilty of *anything*. I'd like to see that footage. I bet you couldn't even see who was driving."

"I never went to the cabin without John. Not until after he died."

"Cameron! Stop talking. Please."

She returned the detective's stare without acknowledging Simon's words.

"In the last few days, is there anything that's come to your mind about your husband that you think I should know?" Mulholland's jaw flexed as he bit down on his gum. "Times he came home late, or trips he took alone? Or with a client? A friend?"

Cameron shook her head. "I'm sorry, but there isn't."

Simon placed a hand on her forearm. "You don't have anything to be sorry about, Cam."

Tears filled her eyes, and she looked away from the two men.

Her eyes rested on the dim blinking red light beyond the mirrored glass wall. She'd never been in an interview room before. Not even when she was questioned by police about her first husband. The memory caused a tightness to form in her chest.

Simon cleared his throat, pulling her back to the present.

"My client has had enough. She's been more than cooperative, and she's had a traumatic few days." He stood, signaling the interview was over. "She needs to rest."

"Wait." Cameron raised her palm toward Simon. "I learned something today. John took out a second mortgage on our home a few months before his death. It was for a million dollars."

She watched the detective's expression as she relayed this information. *Does he already know this?* But his face betrayed nothing.

"*And* he cashed out his life insurance policy two years ago. It was a million-dollar policy, and he surrendered it for less than fifty grand."

Mulholland folded his hands atop the laminate wood table. "Why do you think he did that?"

"That's enough, Detective. She's exhausted." Simon put his hand on Cameron's shoulder. "You don't have to answer that."

Cameron still couldn't tell if this was coming as a surprise to Mulholland or not. "I don't know. Maybe he knew you were coming for him. That he'd be caught eventually. What if—" She glanced at Simon as he sat back down in his metal chair.

"Cam, I was there." Simon's voice was gentle, quiet.

"But you didn't actually see him get taken by the bear."

"I heard him scream. It was gut-wrenching. I saw the tracks. And the blood." He exhaled, and his gaze fell to the table. "I was there."

Cameron faced the detective. "Didn't you think it was strange that he was attacked and never found right before you were planning to arrest him?"

"I didn't quite have enough to arrest him when he disappeared. But yes, I considered that he faked his death."

Simon scoffed. "That's absurd."

Mulholland's gaze didn't waver from Cameron's. "That blizzard moved through the Frank Church Wilderness for two days, which stalled the search. And there's no way he could've survived being out in the elements like that for long, even if he managed to survive the bear attack. The only lodge that was even in the vicinity was the Marble Mountain Lodge where Simon and John were staying. And we know that he didn't show up there. If he was planning to escape, there were better ways than disappearing inside two million acres of federal forest land on the brink of winter."

"You bastard, I heard him scream in agony when those bears attacked!" Simon slapped his palm atop the table, making Cameron jump. "You're insinuating—"

"No, I'm not. I kept an eye on his credit cards and bank accounts—just in case. But there's been no activity. I also put his name on a travel alert. If he *had* somehow survived, there would be a trace. Somewhere. And there isn't."

"Then what about the money?" Cameron asked. "Why did he cash out his life insurance and take out a second loan on our home?"

"I don't know what he used the life insurance payout for, but after looking into the firm's finances, I learned why he took out the second mortgage. And I think Simon here might be able to explain it for us."

Cameron turned to Simon with wide eyes. He grimaced at Mulholland before meeting her eyes.

"The firm was in trouble. Has been for a while. Times have been tough these last few years, and we struggled to keep up appearances. We took the Rothberg case pro bono knowing it would bring John and me national prestige if we won. But we got in over our heads, and we didn't have enough resources to keep building a proper defense."

Cameron's eyes followed Simon's as he stared at the laminate wood table, feeling a familiar stab of betrayal. How was she the last to know about this?

"So, we each took out a second mortgage on our homes. And we used it to create the best defense possible."

There were tears in his eyes when he looked up from the table. "I'm so sorry, Cam. For not telling you. And we never should've gone on that hunting trip. We'd been working so hard on the Rothberg defense. John and I thought the short trip would help clear our minds before the trial. After John's...accident, I planned to repay you for the loan after I won the case. But then I...well, you know."

Cameron stared at Simon. *Did he have no shame?* To keep these kinds of secrets from her after the death of her husband? She couldn't help but feel a token of pity for him, even though his dishonesty still stung. The Rothberg trial had been all over the news. The nation was captivated by the beautiful housewife accused of enlisting her boyfriend to kill her husband for his life insurance money.

John and Simon had been consumed in planning for it for over a year. They were convinced there wasn't enough evidence to convict her. When John went missing one week before the trial started, Simon was forced to try the case alone. And he lost. If the firm was in financial trouble before they took the pro bono case, Cameron could only imagine what shape it was in now.

Simon glared at Detective Mulholland before he laid his hand on top of Cameron's. "I'm sorry for not telling you sooner. I didn't want to do it like this. I was hoping to find a way to repay you, but after I screwed up the case, I'm not sure I'll even be able to repay my own."

Cameron noticed the dark circles under Simon's eyes for the first time. It was impossible to stay mad at him. They were both deceived by John and left to deal with the aftermath of his crimes.

Cameron squeezed his hand. "It's okay, Simon."

"Is there anything else you'd like to tell me?" Mulholland asked.

An image of the house she shared with her first husband—engulfed in flames—filled her mind. She studied Mulholland from across the small table, thinking how different he was to the younger detective who questioned her after Miles's death. There was an intensity in Mulholland's dark blue eyes. She had a feeling he wasn't the type to let things go. "No."

Simon looked across the table. "I think that's enough for one night."

Detective Mulholland pressed his palms against the table. "Of course. I appreciate you coming down tonight, Cameron. And if you think of anything, please let me know."

Cameron nodded before standing, realizing for the first time how exhausted she was. Simon held the door open for her. She felt Mulholland's eyes as the detective followed them down the hall to the elevators.

CHAPTER ELEVEN

Cameron exhaled when the elevator doors closed behind her and Simon. Simon stepped in front of her as they descended to the parking garage. At first, she thought he was going to apologize for not telling her about the firm's financial state, but the look on his face said otherwise.

"Next time, before you start telling the police all of John's financial secrets, tell me first." Simon pointed a finger at his chest. "Then I can decide if it's something we need to tell them. Got it?"

Cameron pursed her lips and pointed a finger at her own chest. "I don't owe John any protection. And you should talk. A little heads-up about my financial devastation would've been nice. Rather than hearing about it in there alongside Mulholland."

"I'm not worried about John. It's *you* I'm trying to protect. I'm the one who's looking out for you. Not them." He moved his pointed finger toward the ceiling of the elevator. "*I'm* the one who's on your side."

Cameron took a step toward him in the small space. "If you were on my side, you would've come clean about the firm—a few months ago instead of now. When I could've actually been able to sell my house!"

The elevator doors opened, and Cameron stormed past him into the cool night air. While she was shocked to learn Simon had known about John's second mortgage, she was relieved she didn't have to share the firm's financial burdens. When Simon and John formed their partnership, years before she and John were married, they'd designated each other as the sole heir to the firm if either of them died. As it turned out, having no stake in the firm was a blessing.

"Cameron, wait! I'm sorry. I know, I should've told you. I was hoping I'd be able to earn it back—for both of us. But then I lost that case. I was just so shaken up by John's death. Now, I'm afraid I'm on the brink of losing everything."

Cameron stopped when she reached her Lexus. She turned around and saw genuine remorse in Simon's eyes. *I know exactly how you feel.* She didn't say it, but he must've read her thoughts.

"Forgive me. That was a stupid thing to say."

"It's okay. Really. This isn't your fault. It's John's."

Simon came toward her. "Did you ever see any signs of John being a killer?"

Cameron thought about the safe distance she and John had established in their relationship. She shook her head. "No. Did *you*?"

He sighed. "No."

"I don't remember driving to Cle Elum or going over the pass when Detective Mulholland saw my car on a traffic cam. Do you think John took my car without me knowing?" But she remembered Mulholland said John was in California.

Simon frowned. "Mulholland could be lying for all we know. To see if you'll disclose more. He doesn't have anything on you."

"What John did was so horrific. How can Detective Mulholland think I would've helped him do that?"

"I think Mulholland was just fishing. Since you were closer to John than anyone."

"I had no idea John was a killer."

"I know." Simon glanced around before reaching into his overcoat pocket. "I have something for you."

He stepped closer to her and pressed a key into her palm. Cameron looked down and saw there was a Post-it note stuck to it. Using his other hand, he closed Cameron fingers around the key.

"It's a safety deposit box." He lowered his voice. "It was John's. He kept this in the safe at the firm. With that recent trial, I forgot about it. I remembered today and thought you better have it in case that detective decides to search the firm."

"They haven't been to the office?"

"Oh, they've been *to* the office, but not in. I might have lost the Rothberg case, Cameron, but I'm not stupid."

Cameron looked at the key in her hand. "What's in it?"

He shrugged. "I have no idea. I can go with you to the bank if you want."

Cameron thought about it for a moment. "That's okay."

Simon nodded and turned for his car. "Call me if you change your mind."

CHAPTER TWELVE

Tanner leaned back in his chair at his cubicle in the Seattle Homicide Unit. It was after eleven. The squad of detectives working the evening shift had all gone home for the night, leaving him alone in the unit.

He took out his tasteless gum and wadded it into a wrapper that he found on his desk. He wondered if Cameron only brought up her husband still being alive to try and throw suspicion off her Lexus being caught on the I-90 traffic camera. Although, Prescott's widow seemed genuinely surprised at her car being on the mountain pass. Tanner couldn't see who was driving, and it was possible John paid an ex-client to take her car with one—or both—of the women in the trunk. But that seemed unlikely without Cameron knowing.

Cameron didn't strike him as the type to help her husband rape and murder other women, but, if she *was* guilty, she wouldn't be the first. Tanner reflected on the infamous Canadian woman who, along with her husband, raped and killed a series of young women in the early nineties, including her younger sister. It wasn't common, but it happened.

When Tanner was still building a case against Prescott, he interviewed some of his clients who'd been in town when the two teachers disappeared. He compiled a list of a dozen people. Some weren't willing to talk to him. Some had alibis. He'd initially suspected Prescott used his life insurance payout as a cash payment to an accomplice. But aside from Prescott withdrawing the fifty grand in cash, Tanner had no evidence, no payments, no trace of any of them helping John.

He leaned forward in his chair and typed Cameron's full name into the Department of Licensing criminal background database. Not surprisingly, she had no arrests or criminal history.

He closed out of the background check and typed Cameron's name into the Accurint database. A list of Cameron's relatives, spouses, and previous addresses appeared. Another spouse was listed beneath John's name. *Miles Henson.*

Tanner hadn't realized she'd been married before John. The marriage only lasted two years. He sat up straight and clicked on the name. A large red *D* popped up on his screen, which meant that Miles Henson was deceased.

Cameron had been living in Sequim, a seaside town two hours west of Seattle, when Miles died. Tanner would have to wait until tomorrow to contact the Clallam County Coroner's Office to request the autopsy report. *If* one had been done.

But Tanner expected there should be one. It wasn't likely that Miles Henson died from natural causes. He was only twenty-nine at the time of his death.

Tanner opened his Internet browser and searched for *Miles Henson Sequim*. An article from the local newspaper topped the search with a photo of a charred home burned down to the studs appearing beside the headline: *SEQUIM DENTIST SETS HOME ON FIRE BEFORE APPARENT SUICIDE.*

Tanner opened the article and pulled a fresh stick of gum from his pocket as he began to read.

CHAPTER THIRTEEN

A sharp rap on her front door startled Cameron awake. She sat up on her living room couch and squinted from the sunlight intruding through her closed curtains. She didn't remember falling asleep.

She raised a palm to her forehead as the obnoxious knocking continued. Her head was throbbing, and her mouth felt dry. Her eyes focused on the empty bottle of Cabernet on the coffee table. Her recollection of last night was foggy, but the suspicions she'd tried to wash away with the dry red came flooding back to her: that John was still alive. That he had planned this.

She reached for her phone, which was almost dead. It was after ten. She had missed calls from Simon and her front office manager. The knocking grew louder, and she groaned as she moved toward the unrelenting noise.

She opened the front door app on her phone, but before it could load, her screen went black. She thrust her phone into a charging dock in the kitchen before returning to her entryway.

She bent to look through the peep hole, guessing it was probably Simon. But it wasn't. It was that same blonde reporter from the other day. She had her microphone clenched in her hand and was practically salivating.

Cameron swore under her breath. *"Go away!"* She turned the deadbolt above the door handle.

The reporter's eyes lit up. "Ms. Prescott! We just want to ask you a few questions about the article that was published this morning. What was it like being married to John? Did you ever have any suspicions that he might be The Teacher Killer?"

"I don't know what article you're talking about. Get off my property or I'm calling the police!" The ferocity in her own voice surprised her.

The reporter pursed her lips and bent down to lift Cameron's morning newspaper off her porch. Although the world had gone digital, John loved the novelty of having the paper delivered every morning. Cameron envisioned him skimming the large pages over a cup of coffee at the kitchen table. She'd kept the subscription after he was gone, finding comfort in the way the daily paper delivery kept John's memory alive.

She made a mental note to cancel it.

"This article."

Cameron's stomach lurched when she recognized her own photo on the cover of *The Seattle Tribune*.

"Please," the reporter continued. "Just one question. Then we'll leave you alone."

"I'm calling the police."

"That's not necessary." Cameron watched the woman raise her hand in the air before pulling something out of her blazer pocket. "I'm just going to leave my card on your porch—in case you want to talk. And you might want to read that article."

"You can keep it. I'm not talking to you."

The reporter dropped it on her welcome mat anyway before turning to follow her cameraman toward the street.

Cameron waited until she couldn't see the reporter anymore before opening the door. The morning light triggered a dull pain inside her head as she reached for the *Tribune*.

"Cameron! Cameron, we want to talk to you! How are you feeling right now? Did you know your husband was a serial killer?"

Cameron lifted her head to see a handful of more reporters standing beyond her wrought iron fence. Two news vans were parked at the curb behind them, along with several cars and a group of onlookers who were holding their phones toward Cameron.

"What do you say about allegations that you were helping him? As his accomplice?"

Cameron swiped the paper off the ground before retreating inside and slamming the door shut. She twisted the lock in the doorknob and turned the deadbolt. She leaned against the door and unrolled the newspaper with trembling hands.

HUMAN REMAINS DISCOVERED AT JOHN PRESCOTT'S CLE ELUM HUNTING CABIN

She skimmed the article, which only detailed what she already knew. Her knees buckled upon seeing a second, slightly smaller headline halfway down the page.

WAS THE TEACHER KILLER'S WIDOW HIS PARTNER IN CRIME?

Below the headline was a photo of Cameron smiling outside her dental practice. Farther down in the article was a smaller photo of her Laurelhurst home. Cameron slid to the floor as she read the article.

It detailed her nearly decade-long marriage to John and speculated how one could be married to a serial killer and not know. It stated that Seattle detectives admitted she was a person of interest in the ongoing investigation. She let the paper fall to the hardwood floor without reading the rest.

After pushing herself to her feet, she stepped over the *Tribune* and grabbed her phone from the charging pad in the kitchen. She pressed Simon's name from her missed call log. He answered after the first ring.

"Cam. I saw the news this morning. Are you all right? I was just about to come over."

"I'm fine. Yes, I just saw it. The reporters are back. Camped out on the street in front of my house."

"Those bastards. Leave it to me. I'll call the station and see if I can convince them to back off. In the meantime, do you have a friend you could stay with?"

"Um." *No*, she thinks. *I have no one.* It struck her that other than John, she had no close friends. Her parents had died in a car accident on their way to her graduation from dental school. An only child, she had needed to handle their funeral arrangements at the same time as interviewing for her first job.

Her first marriage was incredibly isolating. After she married her boyfriend from dental school, he became increasingly possessive of her. Suspicious of any friendships, turning on her with a jealousy that would often turn to rage. It was easier just to avoid any relationships outside their marriage. And after she married John, she'd kept busy with her dental practice, and traveling with him.

"Well, if you need to, you can stay with us. Our remodel won't be finished for a few months, but I'm sure we can find a place—"

"Oh, no. You don't need to do that. I—" She cleared her throat. "I have someone I can call. Yeah."

"Are you sure?"

"I'm sure. Thanks, though."

"All right. I'm going to get to work on pulling those reporters off your street for good. If they so much as set foot on your property again, call me. Right away. Okay?"

"I will. Thank you, Simon."

Her phone rang again as soon as she'd hung up. Recognizing the number, she answered.

"Hi, Daniela." Other than Simon, Daniela was the closest thing to a friend she had.

"Hi, Dr. Prescott." Daniela's normally bubbly voice sounded different than normal. Careful, guarded. "Have you seen the *Tribune* this morning?"

Cameron glanced at the newspaper on her entryway floor. "I have."

"That's kind of why I'm calling." There was relief in Daniela's tone now that she didn't have to relay the headline story to her boss. "I checked our office voicemail this morning and it was full of patients calling to say they're switching dentists. All of our patients for next week have canceled."

Cameron moved across the kitchen. Her throbbing head was in desperate need of coffee.

"Of course they have," she muttered.

She turned on her espresso machine and let out a moan when she saw her grinder was out of beans. She placed the call on speaker, seeing her battery was almost dead again, before rummaging through her pantry.

"Are they afraid I'm going to strangle them in the middle of a filling?"

She was met with silence on the other end of the call.

"But seriously, I'm over being punished for what John did. People are acting like *I'm* The Teacher Killer, you know? And I was wondering, although I know this is a big ask. But the media are camped outside my house and—" On the bottom shelf of her pantry, Cameron found a bag of espresso beans behind an old canister of John's protein powder. "Thank God."

"What?"

"Oh. Sorry. I thought I was out of coffee for a minute." Daniela made the best lattes with their office espresso machine. It made Cameron long for the normalcy of her weekday routine.

"Dr. Prescott, I also needed to call to say I'm sending you my resignation. I'm so grateful to have worked for you these last eight years. It's nothing personal. And I hope this might even lessen your financial burdens right now. So you don't have to keep paying staff when there's no um…" her voice faltered, "patients."

Cameron dropped the bag of coffee beans onto the counter and brought a hand to her face. Why hadn't she seen this coming? Of course, Daniela would resign. Who would want to work for her anymore?

"Thanks for calling to let me know." She tried to contain the wobble in her voice, embarrassed that she assumed they were anything more than employer and employee. "I know an email would have been easier, so I appreciate it."

"I'm so sorry. About everything, Dr. Prescott. You don't deserve this."

Cameron blinked back the tears that erupted in her eyes. She was afraid to respond, knowing her emotion would show.

"What was it you wanted to ask me?"

"Oh." Cameron took a deep breath, hoping to dispel the wave of emotion. "It's nothing." She was grateful she'd at least saved herself the embarrassment of asking to stay at her office manager's house. "It was just work stuff. Can you cancel all our future appointments? Maybe we can mail something to our patients letting them know we've closed. Thank them for their business, let them know how to transfer their records, things like that."

"Of course. But are you sure? I could help you post some job openings if you'd rather?"

"No. I'm sure." With no patients and no staff, she couldn't afford the electricity, let alone the office lease. "Can you call the building manager and let them know we have to break our lease?" She sighed into the phone. "And find out what the penalty is going to be."

"Okay. I'll let you know when that's done."

"Thanks. And I'd be happy to give you a reference for your next job."

"Oh."

An awkward pause filled the call, and Cameron realized the absurdity of her offer. *What good would a reference be from a serial killer's wife?*

"Um. Thank you, that would be great."

"Sure." Cameron ended the call without saying goodbye. She immediately regretted it. Daniela had been a great employee, and she deserved to know how much Cameron appreciated her through the years. But she didn't trust herself to say another word without breaking down into sobs.

Cameron poured the beans into the grinder, spilling extra all over the counter. She wanted to be a dentist for as long as she could remember.

It was her own fault that she had no one to turn to. But the reality of being alone still stung.

She pressed down on the lid of the coffee grinder, letting the shrill noise drown out her thoughts.

CHAPTER FOURTEEN

Cameron cracked the blinds and peered out her upstairs window. The two media vans were still parked on the curb in front of her home, along with a car from the *Tribune*. The number of people standing on her sidewalk had more than doubled. It had been over an hour since she talked to Simon, and she hoped he would have gotten rid of them by now. *Maybe he's drawing up some official legal document to keep them away for good.*

She looked down the street, wishing she could go for a run. Burn off some of the anger that threatened to boil out of her skin. But the media would follow her, which would only make things worse.

After finishing a half pot of coffee, she'd forced herself to get dressed. She turned from the window, grabbing a pair of oversized sunglasses from her dresser. She couldn't stay in this house any longer and be a prisoner for John's crimes.

She peeked through the blinds one last time before going downstairs.

She entered the two-car garage and climbed inside her Lexus. A wave of revulsion ripped through her like an electric current when she eyed John's Range Rover parked beside her. *I'll sell it.* But since John bought it new last year, she'd probably be lucky to get back what she owed.

She pulled the hood of her jacket over her head before opening the garage door. A mechanical hum filled the garage as the door lifted. Cameron checked her rearview mirror before putting her car in reverse. A group of reporters and their camera teams flocked to the end of her drive from the door's motion.

Her jaw tensed. *They better stay out of my way.* Cameron backed up slowly until she saw the reporters gather at the end of her drive, blocking her access to the street.

"Dr. Prescott!" A man held up his arm as Cameron continued to reverse down her drive. "Are you helping the police in their investigation of your late husband? Can you tell us anything about the human remains found at your Cle Elum cabin? Did you have any idea that your husband was The Teacher Killer?"

She locked her doors. She could see the man's facial features clearly in her backup camera as she rolled to a stop a few feet in front of him. A woman shouted more questions at her. None of them made any attempt to move out of her way.

Heat rushed to her face. This is my house. Who are they to keep me here?

The man moved to the side of her car and stopped beside her window, making a motion for her to roll it down.

"Come on! Just answer a few questions. The public has a right to know about your husband. Do the police suspect you were helping him?" He eyed her with disdain, as if she were the one intruding on *his* rights.

Cameron fingered a button on her key fob and tapped it hard to close her garage door. She gripped the steering wheel tighter and checked her backup camera another time before lifting her foot off the brake. None of the other reporters had moved from the end of her drive, but she was beyond caring.

She hit the gas, feeling a rush of satisfaction from the panicked looks on the reporters' faces before they dove out of the way of her retreating car. She heard screams and watched a woman roll onto the sidewalk as her camera fell off the curb and into the street.

The man who'd approached her window ran toward her. "You bitch! You could've killed them!"

"What did you expect!" Cameron screamed back.

He slammed his palm onto her hood seconds before Cameron was jerked forward as a sudden impact forced her car to a stop. She checked her camera screen and saw she'd rear-ended one of the parked news vans.

There was a shrill sound of metal grinding against metal. The reporter's mouth dropped open in shock as Cameron threw her Lexus into drive.

"You're gonna pay for that!" He thrust his palm against her side window before pointing to the van behind her.

Despite what just happened, Cameron's lips turned upward into a smile. "No, I'm not."

It dawned on her that the group of onlookers had probably videoed the whole thing from the adjacent sidewalk. She pressed her foot on the gas before rolling down her window to give the reporters the finger while she sped away from her home.

Cameron parked her car at the Renton Municipal Airport and walked toward the rented hanger. She didn't bother checking the damage to her bumper. The winter air was cool and damp. She stuck her hands in the pockets of her goose down jacket. The sky was overcast, but the visibility was good enough that she would be safe.

On her way here, she'd driven past her dental practice. She wasn't sure why. Maybe as a reminder of when her life was normal, which seemed hard to remember. But seeing the news van parked in the empty parking lot of her practice did nothing but infuriate her. *Why can't they just leave me alone?*

She thought of the three-page article about her and John in that morning's *Tribune*. The media was obsessed now that the police had discovered the identity of The Teacher Killer. They had called John the most infamous serial killer of the Pacific Northwest since Ted Bundy.

She opened the side door to her hangar and flicked on the lights. The sight of her yellow Cessna usually relaxed her, but now, like everything she owned, it was marred with memories of John. After pressing a button on the wall to raise the hangar's main door, she pulled the plane outside. She closed the hangar door and climbed inside her Cessna.

After receiving takeoff clearance from the control tower, she taxied toward the runway and lined up. Cameron glanced at her takeoff checklist before she pushed in the throttle to full power, lifting the plane off the runway before it gave way to Lake Washington. She admired the sapphire water below and ascended above Mercer Island, savoring the feeling of leaving the world, and her problems, behind. She continued to climb in altitude as she flew over the north side of the lake. She turned left for Puget Sound as she soared over the suburbs, wishing she never had to come down.

When she reached the Sound, she followed the water, taking in Whidbey Island on her right. The channel narrowed when she neared Port Townsend, where the Sound opened to the Strait of Juan de Fuca.

When the San Juan Islands appeared on her right, she tilted the yoke to the left and turned the small plane 180 degrees back toward Seattle. If she didn't turn around, in another ten minutes she'd fly over Sequim. And the clearing where the house she'd shared with her first husband had once been.

After crossing the Sound, she flew north of downtown, careful to avoid the restricted airspace that protected the flight paths of commercial jets flying in and out of SeaTac and Boeing Field. Out her side window, Mount Rainier's snow-covered peak protruded beyond the Seattle skyline.

She flew east until the city landscapes changed to evergreen-covered forest. Before she reached the base of the

Cascade Mountains, she climbed in altitude to stay above their pointed tops. Her thoughts were lost in the rugged mountain terrain when she recognized the small town of Cle Elum in the distance.

She drew in a sharp breath and subconsciously searched the mountainside for John's cabin. It took her less than a minute to find it. Through the snow-topped trees, she spotted the disturbance in the snow where the excavators had dug up the bodies.

She stared at the pile of dirty snow piled up beside the hole big enough for two graves. Those poor women, buried outside the cabin, killed in the bed she'd shared with John and slept in almost every weekend since his bear attack.

The media was right. How could she not have even suspected who John was? If she hadn't been so consumed by protecting her own secret, she might have seen John for the monster he was.

Tears blurred her vision as she looked out her side window. Even though she hadn't willingly taken part in John's crimes, was she also to blame?

What happened to John to make him like this? And how evil must he have been to hide it so well? John wasn't a man weighed down by a guilty conscience.

Detective Mulholland implied John's high school English teacher triggered him to kill because of an inappropriate relationship she had initiated. But was that enough to turn John into a sadistic psychopath for the rest of his life? The depravity of his crimes ran deeper than that.

Considering everything she'd learned about him, she wondered if he'd been the one to seduce his teacher. She glanced at her fuel gauge. She had less than an hour of fuel left. She needed to turn back, but she couldn't bear to go home.

She stared out her side window at John's hunting property. The place where she had come to feel close to him. The place that would now haunt her forever.

Everything good in her life was gone. Her gaze shifted across the thick forest that surrounded John's cabin. It would be so easy to end it all. A hard push on the yoke is all it would take.

"*Terrain! Terrain!*" A computerized voice erupted from the overhead speaker and filled the cabin, ripping her out of her thoughts.

Cameron's eyes darted to the windshield. A sheer mountainside was all she could see. She was heading straight for it, so close she could clearly make out a deer navigating a crevasse in the ice.

The alarm continued to flood the small space. "*Terrain, Pull Up! Terrain, Pull Up!*"

If she didn't pull up, she'd crash into the cliff in a matter of seconds. She yanked the yoke toward her and pushed in the throttle as far as it would go. The nose of her Cessna tilted toward the sky. Cameron fell against her seat as the plane climbed toward the mountain's peak.

Her pulse throbbed in her ears. Her plane was only a few feet from the treetops. She pulled back harder as she soared toward the side of the cliff. *I'm not going to make it.* She let out a scream and pulled the yoke as far back as it would go.

The nose lifted so that she was flying almost parallel to the mountainside. *I'm too late.* The rocky boulders that protruded from the snow at the top of the mountain were directly beneath her.

Cameron clutched the yoke toward her chest. Her body tensed, bracing for impact. The nose of the plane ascended the jagged mountaintop with only inches to spare. The plane jerked to the left as her landing gear made contact with the mountain.

The nose dropped and Cameron fought to keep tension on the yoke. The plane bounced hard on the rocky peak. Cameron clenched her teeth as the engine roared and she swerved down the other side of the mountain.

Her heart pounded through the piercing alarm while she stared down at the crater below. With shaking hands, she allowed the yoke to come forward. The plane had leveled. She was out of danger, depending on the damage done from hitting the peak. She strained to see the landing gear out her side window. The wheel on her side was intact, but she could only hope the wheel on the right side and beneath the nose hadn't been bent, or completely torn off.

She breathed through the adrenaline that pumped through her body. Her life was the only thing she had left. She couldn't let John rob her of that, too.

She tilted the yoke to the left, turning the plane back toward Seattle. If John was out there somewhere, he didn't deserve to be alive. He'd taken too much, gone too far. And she couldn't let him win.

Cameron began her second descent over Lake Washington as she approached the Renton airport from the north. She'd already made a distress call to the control tower, who cleared her to do a fly-by so they could assess her landing gear. After flying by the tower, she'd been astonished to learn her landing gear and tires were intact.

She glanced at her purse atop the seat beside her and remembered the safety deposit key Simon gave her last night. *What was John keeping in there? More photos or mementos from his kills?* Part of her didn't want to know. If it was more evidence, she'd have to give it to Mulholland. And it would likely be all over the news tomorrow.

She looked out at the navy lake beneath her and lifted the latch on her side window before pushing it open a few inches. Her hair blew about the small fuselage as she used her other hand to unzip the side pocket of her purse. She withdrew the key and moved it toward the open window.

As she held the key in the air, her curiosity got the better of her. *Maybe there's something in there that could lead to John's accomplice, if he had one.* It might clear her from suspicion. And there were still so many unanswered questions. She thought of the families of John's victims. If there was evidence, they deserved to know.

Renton Tower blared through her headset. "Cessna 4829 Romeo, you are number one and cleared to land on runway three-four."

She tossed the key back inside her purse. "Roger, 4829 Romeo cleared to land on runway three-four."

CHAPTER FIFTEEN

Cameron waited until the bank manager left and she was alone in the safety deposit room at the Pacific Bank. She slid the key into the small metal box. She inhaled a deep breath and stilled her hand before turning it. *Maybe it would be better to never know what was inside.*

Before she could change her mind, she twisted the key and opened the lid to the box. It was empty aside from a red Cartier jewelry box. It looked identical to the one that encased her engagement ring when John proposed.

She hesitated before opening the small square case. John was always a generous gift giver. Was this something he was planning on giving her for Christmas? The thought made her nauseous.

She flipped open the case before she had time to think about it anymore. Instead of jewelry, it contained a single SD card. Just like the one she found at the cabin.

The police headquarters where Mulholland worked was only a few blocks away. *Should I go straight there and give it to him?* But she needed to see it for herself first.

She dropped the electronic storage device into her purse along with the key and headed for the bank door.

Cameron walked slowly back to her car. A growing sense of dread at the thought of returning to her house weighed her down with each step. After getting inside her Lexus, her phone *pinged*. A text from Simon. *I took care of the reporters and the crowd in front of your house. They're all gone. If they come back, call me.*

She wondered what he did to get them to leave but was too exhausted to ask. She started her engine and tossed her phone onto the passenger seat. All that mattered was that they were gone.

Cameron drove under the speed limit after reaching her neighborhood, not having the energy to deal with the media if they'd already come back. A lone, blue Tesla was parked on the curb in front of her house. Cameron checked to make sure her car doors were locked before turning into her drive.

She didn't recognize the car. Whoever it was, she would let Simon take care of it. Cameron pressed the button to close her garage door before she stepped out of her sedan.

"Cameron!"

She turned, remembering the tall red-haired woman who stood in her driveway from yesterday. Cameron pressed the clicker on her key fob and her garage door reversed directions.

"Is this an okay time?" Shay lifted a manila folder in the air.

Cameron stepped toward the rear of her car, seeing the sizable dent in her bumper and missing taillight for the first time. She forced a smile. "Yes, come on in. Sorry, I forgot you were coming back today."

Shay followed Cameron inside through her garage, and Cameron led her to the kitchen table.

"Can I get you anything?"

"Water would be great." Shay removed her leather trench coat and draped it over the back of her chair.

Cameron thought of John's SD card inside her purse and the endless disturbing possibilities of what it contained when she placed her bag on the marble counter. She filled two glasses with water and set them on the table before taking a seat across from Shay.

Shay folded her manicured hands atop the thick stack of papers. "Are you still wanting to sell?"

"Of course. More than ever. I can't stay in this house."

"I understand." She paused to take a sip of her water. "I'm sure you're aware of the article in the *Tribune* this morning."

When Cameron didn't respond, Shay continued. "In light of that, and the article showing a picture of your home, I don't recommend listing this any higher than two point seven. It might be more realistic to price at two point five, but I understand you're wanting to try for a little higher."

Cameron fidgeted in her seat and wrung her hands under the table. If she sold for anything less than three point three, she'd owe money. Money she didn't have.

"But I'm afraid if we list any higher than two point seven, this could sit on the market for a while. And, in the end, that could result in you getting even less than what we're talking about—the two point five."

Cameron closed her eyes, knowing she couldn't bear to live here for much longer. If she sold the plane, her jewelry, furniture, and their art, she could probably pay the difference on the house. She thought of selling the cabin, but quickly remembered it was a crime scene now. *And who would buy it after what happened there?*

"Fine." When she opened her eyes, Shay was staring at her from across the table with wide eyes beneath ornate lashes. "Let's do two point seven."

Shay's expression softened. "Excellent. That's what I've drawn up." She withdrew two pens from her Gucci purse and slid one across the table to Cameron, alongside a small stack of papers.

"Just sign and date on this line." Shay pointed to the bottom of the contract.

She waited for Cameron to finish before turning the page. "Then initial on the bottom of this one and sign and date on the bottom of the next page."

After signing, Cameron set down her pen and stared at the contract until Shay tucked it under her arm and stood. "I'll email you a copy of this from my office."

Cameron started to get up, but Shay insisted on showing herself out. Cameron watched her step over that morning's *Tribune* before she left out the front door.

As soon as the door closed, Cameron slid the SD card out of her purse. She started upstairs for her laptop but turned back for the kitchen. She poured herself a large glass of wine before retracing her steps to the stairs, knowing she'd need a drink if she was going to stomach whatever John kept on this secret memory card.

She found her laptop on the dresser in her guest room and took a drink from her wine before setting down the glass. She opened the laptop and perched on the side of her unmade bed before inserting the memory card. She felt a sense of déjà vu from the night she first stumbled upon his crime scene photos.

She opened the folder and hovered her cursor over the only icon. A video. If it was a video of one of his kills, she didn't want to see it. She'd already seen too much. She bit her lower lip and thought about calling Mulholland. *I don't have to watch this.*

But what if it's something that proves John didn't really do this? Before she could have another thought, she clicked on the thumbnail image and the video began to play.

CHAPTER SIXTEEN

Goosebumps ran down her arms when she recognized herself in the video. The clarity was slightly grainy, but Cameron would never forget what she was doing in that store. She watched her younger self get in line for the cash register, where she had the forethought to pay cash. Her right hand held a gas can and the other a pair of yellow kitchen gloves.

In the righthand corner of the video, the convenience store security footage was timestamped over eleven years ago. One week before Miles died.

She watched the rest of the video, which was only a few minutes long, to make sure there wasn't anything else on the memory drive. She ripped the SD card out of her computer before marching into the bathroom and flushing it down the toilet, giving it a second flush for good measure.

With the toilet water still churning, she sank to the tile floor and pulled her knees into her chest. How could John possibly have known what she did? The police never even found that footage. She'd worn a baseball hat and paid cash.

As she thought about it, it wasn't that surprising John had this evidence on her. He enjoyed the investigative side of helping his clients. He never left a stone unturned, which was what made him so damn good at what he did.

Cameron stared at the toilet which had now gone quiet. What worried her the most about John having this video was that if he could find it, then Mulholland could too.

Cameron stared at John's empty mahogany bookcase in his home office. The CSI team had left his books piled in several stacks on the floor.

She was still shaken up by the video. Once she was able to bring herself to get up from the bathroom floor, she slid off her wedding ring and listed it on eBay. Tomorrow, she would call the downtown Steinway piano gallery and see what they would give her for John's baby grand. Then, she'd have to sell the Cessna.

She reached for a stack of vintage hunting magazines, remembering how John used to talk about how much they were worth. John would have hated the haphazard way they'd been tossed onto the floor by the crime scene investigators, left in a messy stack that leaned to the side. Some were nearly one hundred years old, but John had kept them in near-perfect condition. She turned and sat in the leather seat behind John's desk.

She flipped through the magazines, wondering what she was expecting to find. It's not like John would have circled on a map where he planned to live out his days after evading the law.

John had hinted through the years about wanting to live off-grid. Self-sustained. He tolerated the city, but he loved escaping to his cabin. Or a remote hunting trip. Unlike Cameron, he was comfortable in isolation.

She went back to the bookshelf and grabbed one of his newer hunting magazines. It opened to an advertisement for guided winter trapline hunts in interior Alaska, starting at $10,000. She flipped to a page with a snow-covered mountain top and noticed a crease in the top right-hand corner. It was no longer folded over, but it once had been. Cameron studied the article. The decorative font of the title, "Yukon-Charly Rivers" caught her eye, along with a photo of a frozen river winding between two peaks. John had gone hunting in Alaska a few times during their marriage.

Goosebumps formed on her arms beneath her sweater. She looked around the office. *Would John have left hidden cameras?* Could he be watching her?

She shook the thought away. If there had been cameras, the police would have found them. *Right?*

She closed the magazine and hurried out of John's office to get her laptop.

Half an hour later, she reclined on her guest bed as she scoured the Internet search results for *Teacher Missing in Alaska.* The most recent articles headlined a teacher missing after an avalanche near Wasilla, and another whose fishing boat capsized last summer. Cameron scrolled through the first page of results. The next few headlines detailed a hiker found alive after being reported missing. There was nothing relevant since John's disappearance.

Cameron felt her bare ring finger with her thumb before typing new search terms: *teacher murdered Alaska*. A headline caught her eye at the top of the results: *Missing College Student's Body Found After Leaving Bar in Tok.*

Cameron opened the article, dated November 24 of last year. Cameron held her breath as she read the first part of the article:

> *The remains of Bethany Long, a twenty-two-year-old education major, have been discovered in the woods less than two miles from where she was last seen leaving her shift at the Wolf Pack Bar in Tok, Alaska.*

Ed major. Cameron reached for her wineglass without taking her eyes off the screen. She replaced it on her bedside table after lifting the empty glass to her lips.

> *Her death has been ruled a homicide by the State Medical Examiner's Office, who said she died by strangulation. Bethany Long was working at the bar while studying online to fulfill her dream of becoming a high school English teacher.*

Cameron's breath caught in her throat. *Just like John's first victim.*

Her friends and family describe her as a bright-spirited young woman who stayed out of trouble. Her car was still parked at the bar when she failed to show up for her shift the next day. The investigation into her death is still ongoing.

The article went on to employ the public to come forward with any leads relating to the night she was last seen. Cameron searched the girl's name for more recent articles, but there was nothing. She typed *teacher killer victims* in a new search and found a recent article with photos of all the women John killed.

Unlike Cameron, all the women had dark hair and olive skin. She wasn't sure if she should be relieved or insulted that she was apparently never John's type. Cameron stopped when she came to the photo of John's first victim, Bethany Valdez, his substitute English teacher. She was young, only twenty-five when she died, and her long black hair and brown eyes bore a striking resemblance to Bethany Long. Along with sharing the same name, they looked like they could have been sisters.

She closed her laptop and covered her mouth with her hand. She crossed the room and reached for her phone perched atop her dresser. It was three-thirty in the morning. But this was too important to wait.

She found Detective Mulholland's number in her recent call log and put her phone to her ear as it rang.

CHAPTER SEVENTEEN

Tanner woke to the familiar sound of his ringtone. He wasn't on call, but he'd left his phone on anyway. It was dark when he rolled over in bed and lifted his phone from his nightstand. Cameron Prescott's name appeared on his phone screen. He glanced at his digital clock. Three-thirty in the morning. He had been dead asleep, for the first time in weeks.

He cleared his throat before answering. "Detective Mulholland."

"Oh, hi. This is Cameron Prescott. I wasn't sure if you'd answer. I'm sorry to call you so late."

Tanner sat up in bed. "That's all right."

"Um. I just wanted to tell you that I think I know where John is."

Tanner rubbed his eyes. "What? What do you mean?"

"I think he's in Alaska. I just read in the news that a young woman was murdered in Tok last November. It's this tiny town between Anchorage and Fairbanks. Anyway, she wasn't a teacher. But she was an education major—wanted to be a high school English teacher—and she was strangled. And she looked exactly like John's English teacher that he killed. Her name is also Bethany."

She paused, then continued when Tanner didn't respond.

"John has always dreamed of living off grid. Alaska would be the perfect place for him to disappear. And this woman was killed less than a month after John's supposed bear attack."

Tanner wondered if she had been drinking. Her words weren't slurred, but she sounded erratic. Did she really think this woman's murder could be connected to her dead husband, or was she trying to distract him from suspecting her as John's accomplice?

"Maybe you should get some sleep," he said.

She sighed into the phone. "You don't believe me."

"I think you've been through a lot.

"We can talk in person later today, if you'd like," he added. "There is something I'd like to ask you about."

"About John?"

"Not exactly."

"Why don't you ask me now?"

He thought about her first husband's autopsy report. His death had been ruled a suicide by a self-inflicted gunshot wound less than twenty-four hours after his death. There'd been hardly any investigation. According to Cameron's statement, her husband had a drinking problem and undiagnosed depression. And he'd refused to get help. "I'd rather speak in person."

"Okay."

"Talk to you tomorrow."

"Detective?"

"Yeah?"

"I know you don't think it's possible. But John's still alive. I can feel it."

I can feel some things too, he thought. *She certainly knows that her first husband is dead.*

"Good night, Cameron."

"Good night, Tanner."

CHAPTER EIGHTEEN

Cameron slid her accent chair out of the way for the three men carrying the piano through her living room. After she called this morning, the downtown Steinway & Sons offered to pick up the baby grand and pay her immediately.

It was worth a lot more than the twenty-five thousand they were giving her, but she was glad for the cash and to be rid of John's prized instrument.

"Good morning."

She turned toward the familiar voice. Detective Mulholland stood in her open front doorway holding that morning's paper in his hand, reminding Cameron she still needed to cancel her *Tribune* subscription. He stepped aside as the piano movers tilted the baby grand and carefully moved through the doorway.

He reappeared as the movers carried the piano down her driveway. "May I come in?"

"Sure."

It was just after ten a.m.. He was impeccably dressed in a blue pin-striped suit. As he handed her that morning's paper, she noticed that he looked fresh as a daisy, no trace of dark circles around his eyes from her calling him in the middle of the night.

Cameron knew from her quick check in the mirror that morning that her own eyes were bloodshot and puffy from the wine she consumed before calling Mulholland. She managed to sleep for only a few hours afterward. She hadn't even bothered with makeup, knowing it wouldn't do much good.

He closed the door behind him.

"Want to have a seat?" She pointed to her living room sofa.

"Yes, thank you."

She glanced at the front-page headline of *The Seattle Tribune* as Mulholland followed behind her.

TEACHER KILLER'S WIDOW PUTS LAURELHURST HOME ON THE MARKET

Why was the media set on ruining her life? She tossed the paper onto her coffee table before plopping down into her zebra-print Edwardian armchair.

"Sorry I woke you in the middle of the night," she said, as he sat down across from her.

"It's no problem." He appeared to mean it.

Cameron moved her thumb across the groove on her ring finger where her wedding ring used to be. She glanced at Mulholland's left hand and noticed he wasn't wearing a ring either. His eyes traveled to the small, framed photo on the end table beside her. She followed his gaze to the picture of her standing between her parents on a backpacking trip in the Olympic Mountains—one of the last photos they'd taken together before their fatal accident.

"Do you have kids?"

"No," he said without hesitation.

This is no family man, Cameron thought. He lives and breathes his work.

She wondered why he was here. "Are you going to look into the woman who was found in the woods near Tok?"

"I spoke with an Alaska state trooper this morning about the case."

Cameron suddenly felt more awake. "And?"

"Less than a year ago, the body of a female tourist was found in that same woods. A few miles away. Her murder is still unsolved, and the local authorities think the two cases might be connected."

"Was this tourist found naked and strangled?"

"No. She was shot."

"Was she a teacher?"

Mulholland shook his head. "She was a recently retired nurse. And neither of these women have the markings of a letter grade like the rest of John's victims."

"John's smarter than that. The world thinks he's dead. John would want to keep it that way. Is there any DNA they can test against John's?"

"No. There was evidence of a sexual assault on the more recent victim, but the killer used a condom. No other foreign DNA on either of the bodies."

"Can you send them John's photo and see if anyone remembers seeing him before this student went missing?" According to her quick Internet search, Tok had a population of around 1800 people. Surely someone would remember an outsider hanging around town, especially the local bar.

"The night Bethany Long went missing after her shift, the bar was packed. There was a major dog sled race the next day. Apparently, it was the first time the town held a race in November. Usually, it's in March."

Cameron remembered seeing something online about Tok being called the dog mushing capital of Alaska.

"The patrons that night were mostly tourists," he continued. "Out of towners. There were only two locals in the whole place, who both admitted to getting hammered before leaving the bar. And John's photo is already all over the news. If someone recognized him, I think they would've come forward by now."

"But...." Why can't he see it? Those cases aren't connected. The second woman was killed by John.

"Look, neither of these women were killed by John. They don't fit with his other kills. *And* if there was any likelihood of John still being alive, he wouldn't have been declared dead."

Cameron couldn't think of anything to say that might convince him otherwise.

"But the reason I came here was to ask you about your first husband."

Cameron sat up straight, trying to hide the ripple of fear that shot down her spine. "What does he have to do with anything?"

"First of all, I want to express my condolences for your having to deal with the deaths of not only one, but two spouses." Cameron watched Mulholland's jaw flex as he chewed a piece of gum. "Would you mind telling me what happened the night of your first husband's death?"

I should call Simon. He would be livid if he found out she was speaking to Mulholland without him. But she didn't want to risk appearing guilty. She inhaled a large breath. *Just keep calm.*

"It's something I try not think about. I'm sure you can look up what happened."

"I did. But I want to hear your perspective."

"Why?"

"Well, there didn't seem to be much of an investigation. His death was immediately ruled a suicide by the county coroner based on the close-range gunshot to his head, but most of the evidence was destroyed in the fire. According to your statement, you weren't home when it happened. I wondered if you felt there was an ample investigation into Mr. Henson's death."

Cameron shifted in her chair.

"I mean, there was never a formal diagnosis of depression or any other mental illness. But you said in your statement he'd had a drinking problem?"

He can't know anything other than what the police report showed. "He did, yes. A lot of dentists are depressed, as I'm sure you've heard before. We were only a couple of years out of dental school when he took his life. I noticed him becoming depressed soon after we started our practice. He never sought help, although I encouraged him to." She sighed, remembering all the nights Miles would get drunk and violent. The time he shoved her down their flight of basement stairs played like a horror movie in her mind. She blinked the memory away. "It was a terrible shock when he killed himself. But not entirely surprising."

Mulholland moved his gum to the other side of his mouth. "And you weren't home when it happened?"

A seagull squawked outside her front window.

There's no way he can prove I was there. "I'd just run to the store for a few things."

"Did Miles ever hurt you?"

Cameron's mouth fell open at the question. She pulled her lips together and shook her head. "No."

He nodded. Did he believe her? She remembered the marathon photos that came up in her Internet search of the detective last night when she couldn't fall asleep after they spoke. In the pictures, the look on his face as he neared the finish line was one of fierce determination. *Someone who doesn't like to lose.*

Her eyes locked with his before he stood to his feet. A sense of dread filled her stomach like a ton of bricks. *He's not going to let this go.*

"Thanks for your time."

"Of course." She followed him toward the door.

He pivoted when they reached the entryway. "Where did you say you found those crime scene photos again, that John took at the cabin?"

"On a bookshelf. I was just looking through some of his old books."

"Yes, that's right. It's somewhat surprising to me that John would leave something like that lying around. It just seems a little...careless."

Cameron crossed her arms.

"Anyway, the medical examiner has positively ID'd the two bodies we recovered from your Cle Elum property. As I suspected, they're the two Seattle teachers who went missing the summer before last." He opened her door but paused before stepping outside. "I might need to speak with you again, so I'd appreciate you letting me know if you're going out of town."

Cameron watched him walk to his car and saw that despite Simon's efforts, the two familiar news vans had returned. She twisted the deadbolt after closing the door and hurried into the kitchen to get her purse.

When she lifted her phone off the counter, she saw her wedding ring had sold on the online auction site she listed it on, which meant she could afford to hold on to her Cessna for a while.

She searched for the phone number of the family-owned convenience store where she'd been caught on camera buying the supplies to burn down the house in Sequim. But the store was now a gas station chain. She dialed the number anyway.

A girl answered the phone, sounding no more than eighteen.

"Hi, I was wondering how long you keep your store's surveillance footage for? Do you still have any of your security videos from ten or eleven years ago?"

"Um…no. We only keep our security footage for like ninety days. After that it gets erased."

Cameron sank against her kitchen cabinets. "Okay." She should have known they wouldn't keep decade-old security footage. While it was a relief, it was also horrifying to know John had kept this footage all these years—for as long as they'd known each other.

"Is this the police or something?"

"Thanks so much." Cameron ended the call and headed out of her house.

Cameron lowered her fur-lined hood and checked her reflection in her compact mirror. It took her a moment to recognize herself. She'd used her kitchen shears to cut her long hair into a blunt bob. The box of hair dye she purchased at the supermarket had transformed her blonde hair into a vibrant carrot red, close to the color of her realtor's.

The shade was a sharp contrast to her green eyes. After penciling in her eyebrows, the color almost looked natural.

She stepped out of the Uber at the Renton Municipal Airport. She hoped leaving her car at home would delay Mulholland—and the press—from finding her. After his last visit to her home, she couldn't stop worrying how far he'd probe into Miles's death.

She thought of the gas-station footage John had been keeping in his safety deposit box. He was always the careful planner. Why? Why had he even married her if he knew? How did John think that video was an advantage?

There was only one way to find out.

She retrieved her duffel bag from the backseat of the car, hoisted it over her shoulder, and headed toward her hangar as a light mist fell from the February sky.

CHAPTER NINETEEN

Cameron looked out the passenger-side window at the thick evergreen forest that lined the two-lane Alaska Highway. The spruce trees were much smaller than the ones she was used to in Washington. They reminded her of a Christmas tree farm. She'd expected everything in Alaska to be bigger, but she wondered if their short stature had something to do with the extreme cold.

"Where did you fly in from?"

She turned to the older man who insisted on giving her a ride to her motel from the Tok Junction airstrip. She planned to get an Uber or a taxi, but the airport manager informed her there was no such thing in Tok and offered to give her a ride. Cameron rubbed her gloved hands together. According to her new phone, it was five degrees Fahrenheit. Despite the warm air blowing through the Ford truck's air vents, she was still freezing.

"Portland." It took her two full days of flying to get to Tok from Seattle, with an overnight stop in Canada, which gave her plenty of time to think about what she would tell people. She couldn't go around asking people to help her find her dead serial killer husband, especially when the media was accusing her of helping him.

Up ahead, Cameron saw a decorated wood cross at the base of a tree beside the road. As the truck sped past it, Cameron recognized the face of the young murder victim on the framed photo that was tied to the tree. Cameron stared out the window. They must be close to where Bethany's body was found.

"So, what brings a woman like you up here?" The sleeves of the man's flannel shirt were rolled up near his elbows. Cameron had no idea how he could stand the weather without so much as a coat.

A woman like me? Cameron glanced at her fur-trimmed coat and heeled boots. *Do I stand out that much?* "I'm going on a trapline hunting trip. It's not until next week, but I've always wanted to come to Alaska."

The driver raised his eyebrows and turned to her. Cameron wished he would keep his eyes on the snow-covered highway.

"*Hunting?* Not by yourself."

Cameron couldn't tell if it was a statement or a question. "No. I'm going with a guide. Tanana Valley Outfitters." She quoted the name of the closest hunting outfitter to Tok, based on her Internet research.

"Oh, yeah. I've heard of them. Never known a woman to come up alone for that kind of thing, though. And a week is a long time to see Tok. You can drive through the whole town in two minutes."

"I want to get to know the place. My grandfather worked at the U.S. Customs Office here in Tok for a short time in the fifties. He used to tell me stories about the place. So, I came early to see the town."

He shot her an inquisitive glance. "What do you do in Portland?"

She'd thought about this too during her flight north. "I'm an accountant for Sovas." Founded in Portland, Sovas had become one of the country's biggest tech giants in the last few years.

"Oh." The airport manager nodded his apparent approval of her made-up occupation.

Cameron looked straight ahead, impressed by the white mountain range in the distance that dwarfed the surrounding forest.

"That's the Alaska Range. Beautiful ain't it?"

The trees cleared and a small stretch of one-story buildings lined the road.

He took a sharp right off the highway. Cameron pressed her hand against the passenger door to steady herself. The truck came to an abrupt stop in front of a log cabin. Beside it, an unlit sign stood slightly taller than the building. *The Howling Wolf Motel: Vacancy.*

Cameron looked out the window. "Oh. We're here already?" They couldn't have been driving for more than a few minutes. "I hadn't expected it to be so close to the airport."

"Everything's close in town." The man lifted Cameron's duffel bag out of the back seat before she could get her seatbelt off. He set it on the seat between them.

"Thank you."

He nodded. "Good luck on your hunt."

"Thanks for the ride." She offered him a smile before opening her side door.

"You're welcome. Good to meet you, Shay."

The cold air hit her when she stepped out of the truck. The truck pulled back onto the highway just as soon as Cameron shut the door. Despite her down coat and gloves, she was chilled to the core. She exhaled a puff of white and pulled her faux fur lined hood over her head.

A bell rang when she opened the door to the motel. A gray-haired woman looked up from behind the large wood counter against the far wall. She wore no makeup, and her hair was pulled into a short ponytail at the nape of her neck. She eyed Cameron as though she were lost.

"Can I help you?" Her voice was deeper than Cameron expected.

Cameron tried not to stare at the large moose head hanging on the wall above the woman's head as she moved toward the counter. "I need a room."

"Sure. How many nights, sweetheart?" A rectangular pin on the woman's sweater read *Manager*.

Cameron set her duffel bag down on the floor. "Four, maybe five."

"Is it just you, hun?"

Cameron forced a smile. "Just me."

"You got it." The woman turned and grabbed a key off the wall behind her. She slid the large, numbered keychain across the counter. "It's one-forty a night, including tax."

"Oh." That was more than she'd expected, but she tried to conceal her surprise. "I'll pay cash." She pulled six one-hundred-dollar bills from the envelope in her bag that she withdrew after the sale of her wedding ring.

"Okay, but I'll still need to have a credit card on file."

Cameron lifted her wallet, thinking she should've known better. This was a small town, sure, but not the 1940s. "Of course." She forced a smile and handed the manager a Visa, figuring there was no outrunning Mulholland anyway. If he wanted to know where she was, he would find her. And, unless he had a warrant for her arrest, he shouldn't be able to stop her.

"I'm Valerie. Just let me know if you need anything during your stay. What brings you to Tok?"

Cameron exhaled in relief when the woman handed her back her card without seeming to recognize her name.

"I'm going on a guided hunting trip. A winter trapline hunt."

The motel manager's eyes widened as they drifted to the fur lining on Cameron's coat. "Is that so? I'm a hunter myself. What are you hoping to trap?"

Cameron thought back to the photos she'd seen on the guided outfitter's website. "Lynx. I have a hunting cabin back home, and I'm hoping to um…" Cameron couldn't imagine killing an animal, even a beast, for no other purpose than a trophy. But apparently, there were people who took joy in it.

She glanced at the moose head on the wall above the manager's head. "Mount one on the walls."

Valerie smiled broadly. "Oh, that's wonderful. And you've come to the perfect place."

Cameron forced herself to return the manager's beaming smile.

"I didn't catch your name, dear."

"Oh. It's Shay." If Valerie noticed the name on her credit card was different from the one Cameron gave her, she didn't show it. Given the woman's sudden warmth, she decided to ask about Bethany. "I saw a photo of a young woman on the side of the road on the way here. It looked like a memorial."

Valerie's smile vanished. She set Cameron's receipt on the counter in front of her. "Oh, yes. Her poor parents and younger sister were utterly devasted."

"What happened?"

The older woman's lips pursed into a hard line. "She went missing one night after her shift at the Wolf Pack Bar. A few days later, her body was discovered in the woods, behind where you saw her photo on the side of the road."

Cameron knew the story, but out of this woman's mouth, it seemed way more real. "Oh, my—"

"She was murdered. And the police still don't know who did it."

"That's awful."

The creases around the motel manager's eyes deepened. Cameron guessed the woman was younger than she looked. While she was pleasant looking, you could tell that she'd lived. She didn't try to mask it, unlike many of Cameron's patients, who froze their face with Botox after turning forty so you couldn't see any real expression.

The manager pointed to the number on Cameron's keychain. "You're number four. Around back, first cabin on the right. The code for the WiFi is on the back of the key."

Cameron slipped her Visa back inside her wallet. "Thank you." She turned and stopped when her eyes met those of a gigantic taxidermied wolf mounted beside the front door. Its mouth was open, exposing the dead animal's large white fangs.

"I shot her myself. Beautiful, isn't she?"

Cameron turned toward the motel manager with wide eyes. "I didn't know wolves were that big." It was larger than the mountain lions she'd seen at the Woodland Park Zoo. The ferocity of its bared sharp fangs sent goosebumps up her arms.

"The wolves in the lower forty-eight are nothing like the ones up here. The farther north you go, the bigger they get. Maybe you'll be lucky enough to trap one on your trip." She pointed to the beast directly behind Cameron. "She was nearly one hundred and eighty pounds. A record in Southeast Fairbanks County."

Cameron looked back at the huge creature. "Was it here? In Tok?"

"No. But they're around here. I shot this one northeast of here, near Eagle. It's closer to the Canadian border. The one in your room is a little smaller, but not much."

My room? Cameron turned to see if the woman was joking, but Valerie's face showed no hint of a smile. Cameron did her best to suppress the shudder that ran through her body.

She started for the door, but Valerie continued.

"I might get a chance to go hunting again soon. There's been reports of rabid wolves in the Yukon-Charley Rivers area northeast of here. Wolves infected with rabies are much more likely to attack subspecies—and humans—so the state might open aerial hunting of them. The disease throws them into a violent rage. And what's more…they lose their fear of people."

Am I giving off a vibe that says I'm dying to know about wolves? "Hope there's none of those around here," Cameron said.

"Not yet, anyway."

Cameron tore her eyes away from the beast and glanced at Valerie before opening the door. For the first time since Cameron asked about Bethany, the woman's smile had returned.

CHAPTER TWENTY

Cameron had only stayed in her tiny cabin long enough to drop off her bag, use the bathroom, and throw a sheet over the massive scowling wolf mounted beside the wall. She didn't know how anyone could sleep with a dead animal's eyes bearing into them, its fangs out like that. Like it might come alive in the night.

"Hey, Shay!" Valerie leaned her head out the motel's office door as Cameron trudged through the parking lot. "You want to borrow a snowmachine?"

Cameron glanced at the big black and green snowmobile parked in the spot reserved for the manager. It looked fast. And dangerous. "No, but thank you. I've never been on one before."

"Oh my, I've been riding one since I was three. That's my new Thundercat 9000. Fast as hell. And heated handlebars. You sure?"

"Thanks, but I'm just going down to the Wolf Pack."

"Oh, all right. Have one for me then!"

Valerie went back inside, and Cameron continued toward the bar. Fortunately, the town was tiny. But even walking a few blocks in the sub-zero temperature chilled her to her bones.

Despite her leather gloves, Cameron's fingertips were numb when she reached the Wolf Pack Bar a few blocks down the Alaska Highway. *Is everything in this town named after wolves?* Her lips quivered from the cold as she opened the log cabin's front door. She stomped the snow off her Sorels before going inside.

"What can I get for you?" a woman with short dark hair asked when Cameron took a seat at the bar.

Cameron tried to keep her teeth from chattering as she read through the beers listed on the lit-up dry erase board on the far wall.

"I'll have an Alaskan White."

"You got it." The woman returned a moment later with an overflowing mug.

Cameron half-expected the bartender to ask what she was doing here but was relieved when the woman turned, leaving Cameron alone with her drink. An hour later, Cameron took the last sip from what was left of her beer. Aside from the elderly man a few stools down from her who'd been splitting his attention between Cameron and the ice hockey game playing on the flatscreen, she was the only patron at the bar. She checked the time on her Tiffany watch. The old man noticed, and his stare drifted uncomfortably from the hockey game to Cameron.

She stared at a poster of Bethany on the wall behind the bar. An Alaska State Trooper badge was printed on the poster's upper left-hand corner. *SEEKING INFORMATION: Homicide Victim Bethany Long* was typed in bold letters above her smiling photo. There was a phone number at the bottom of the poster. Above it, a ten-thousand-dollar reward was offered for information leading to an arrest.

"What's a pretty woman like you doin' up in these parts?"

Cameron turned toward the man who swayed atop his padded barstool two seats down from her own. His words were slurred, and it wasn't even four in the afternoon. His cheek bulged from a wad of chewing tobacco. Cameron watched him spew his dip spit into his empty glass before turning back to her own.

She wondered if he was one of the two locals Mulholland had mentioned who got drunk here the night Bethany disappeared after her shift.

"Leave her alone, Karl."

The bartender tossed a rag over her shoulder and moved behind the counter toward Cameron. "You want another?" She tilted her head toward Cameron's empty beer.

Cameron looked up at the woman, who managed to appear both matronly and tough, guessing she was close to sixty.

"No, thanks." Cameron shot a glance at the old man, glad to see his attention had returned to the TV. "Did you know that woman?" Cameron pointed to the poster on the wall.

The bartender's expression grew serious. "I did. Why are you asking about her?"

Cameron debated what to say. "I saw her photo on the side of the road on my way into town. My motel manager said she was murdered."

"You a reporter?"

"No. I'm an accountant."

The woman folded her arms.

"I'm going on a guided trapline hunt in the area next week," Cameron added.

"*Hmmph.*" The woman dropped her gaze. "Yes, I knew her. She worked here. I was out sick the night she went missing. I'll never stop feeling guilty about it. There was a big dog sled sprint the next day. This place was busy. Mostly out-of-towners."

Karl hollered at the TV. Out the corner of her eye, Cameron saw him nearly fall off his barstool.

The bartender ignored him. She pulled the rag off her shoulder and wrung it between her hands. "I hate to think of Bethany walking to her car that night. Alone. The police think that's probably when she was picked up by her killer." There were tears in her eyes when she met Cameron's gaze.

"She was a beautiful girl."

The woman nodded. "Smart too. Her poor parents. They still come in from time to time. It breaks my heart to see them. Her younger sister too."

The woman's eyes moved toward the chime that resounded from the front door being opened. Cameron turned and watched a tall Alaska state trooper in a blue uniform walk into the bar.

"Hey, Sergeant," the bartender said.

"Hi, Joan."

He gave Cameron a wide berth and took a seat on the other side of Karl.

Joan moved toward him, tossing the rag over her other shoulder. "Thought you were heading up to the lake to check on George today."

The trooper took off his hat and set it on the counter, exposing his thick black hair. "I was, but last weekend's storm blew a bunch of trees down across the trail headed up there. Morris was gonna fly me, but his plane's battery went bad. He's driving up to Fairbanks to get a new one."

"What about Larry? Can't he fly you up there?"

Cameron leaned over the counter to get a better look at the trooper. She guessed he was a few years older than her. She took in his defined jaw and high cheekbone from the side. If he noticed her staring, he didn't show it.

"He flew to Homer yesterday to visit family."

"What about Marty?"

"He's working for the next couple of days." The Alaska trooper rested his elbows on the counter and leaned forward. "I'm worried about him, Joan. He isn't answering his sat phone. I just hope he hasn't had another heart attack. He shouldn't be up there this time of year. But he's so stubborn."

Joan gave him a motherly pat on the arm. "I'm sorry, Sarg. Maybe you can get up there tomorrow?"

He shook his head. "There's another storm coming in tomorrow. If I can't get there tonight, I'm not sure when I'll be able to. I might even have to call an emergency rescue team. But I hate to do that when he could be just not answering his phone." The sergeant let out a deep sigh.

Karl looked up from his beer glass. "I've told you you're welcome to borrow my plane anytime, Sarg. It's even got skis on."

"Thanks, Karl." The trooper patted the old man on the back. "But I'm afraid I need a pilot."

"I'm a pilot," Karl slurred.

"He needs one who isn't on their fifth beer," Joan said.

"I'm a pilot."

The sergeant and Joan both turned at the sound of Cameron's voice. Karl smiled at her through yellowed teeth, as if she were speaking only to him.

"I can take you," she added.

Joan pulled the rag off her shoulder and swatted the sergeant's forearm with it. "There you go."

CHAPTER TWENTY-ONE

"I really appreciate this." The Sergeant moved a couple of apples from the front passenger seat of his Ford SUV before Cameron climbed in beside him.

D. WASKA was embroidered in yellow near the right shoulder of his navy-blue vest. After some not-so-subtle encouragement from Joan, he had reluctantly accepted her offer to fly him to the lake.

"It's no problem."

"I'm Dane, by the way." He held an apple out to her. "You want one?"

Cameron's initial reaction was to decline, but she hadn't eaten since she took off from northern British Columbia that morning. "Sure. Thanks. And I'm Shay." She was getting used to going by her realtor's name. The new hair color helped.

He placed the other apple inside a cupholder. A dispatcher crackled through the police scanner mounted to his dash. Dane listened for a moment before he turned down the volume.

"I thought cops only ate donuts."

A dimple appeared on the side of his cheek when he smiled. "I try to eat healthy when I'm on the job."

Even through his uniform, she could tell he was fit. Cameron pulled her seatbelt across her body.

The sergeant pulled onto the highway toward the airport. "What are you in town for?"

"Oh, I'm going on a guided hunting trip. I'm hoping to trap a lynx and have it mounted in my cabin back in Washington."

"What outfitter are you using?"

She repeated the name of the guide from John's hunting magazine that she'd told to the airport manager.

"Yeah, I know them," Dane said. "You know if you're going with Adam, or Jack?"

Cameron felt his eyes on her but kept her gaze on the road. She bit her lip. "I booked it a while back, but I think it's Jack."

"And you came by yourself?" He raised his eyebrows.

"Yeah." She turned to him. "How long of a flight is it? I doubt Karl's Maule has instruments to fly in the dark."

"It's about half an hour. We should have just enough daylight to make it there and back."

"You said it's on a lake? How close to the airport?"

Cameron turned to him as she waited for his answer.

"The lake *is* the airport." His dark eyes met hers before returning to the road. The sides of his mouth upturned, like he was amused by her question. "It's frozen, solid. You okay with landing on the ice?"

Cameron stared out the windshield. The sun neared the top of the mountain range in the distance. "With the skis on Karl's plane we should be fine. Although, I've never done it before."

"The locals do it all the time. But if you're not comfortable...."

Cameron turned to him. His jaw muscles clenched as he looked out at the two-lane highway. He seemed so worried about George, whoever he was. And getting the sergeant alone in the plane for a half hour was her best chance to ask him about Bethany. "No, that's fine." She tried to sound confident. "It can't be that different." At least, she hoped not.

Cameron lifted the nose of Karl's Maule taildragger off the runway and ascended above the Alaska Highway, aware of the sun nearing the horizon on her left.

"Was that your yellow Cessna parked toward the front of the airport?" Dane asked through the mouthpiece of his headset.

Cameron was busy looking over the instrument panel. It wasn't too different than the Cessna, but she had to focus. "Yep."

"Nice plane."

According to the GPS, they'd reach the lake in a half hour. It would give them less than twenty minutes to check on George if they wanted to make it back before dark. Before takeoff, Dane had set a cooler and a backpack on the plane's backseat.

"Thanks again for taking me," he added.

"You're welcome. It sounds like you're pretty worried about this guy."

"I am. He's too old to be up there alone this time of year."

To Cameron, the trooper seemed to be taking the old man's independence a little too personally.

"He had a heart attack last summer, so who knows…" Dane continued.

As she flew north over the Tanana River, the snow-blanketed spruce trees grew smaller with their increasing altitude. The vast forest beneath them was exactly the sort of place where John could be hiding. There was nothing but wilderness for as far as she could see. Although, she hadn't seen a single building since they left Tok, only dense trees.

"Does anyone live out here? It looks pretty isolated."

"No, this is all state forest around us. There are a few lakes around, but most aren't accessed by roads, so there aren't very many cabins on them. George and I own the only two on Hunt Lake."

"What about farther north?"

"There's not much between here and the Yukon-Charly Rivers Preserve—other than a lot of inaccessible wilderness area."

"Don't people have hunting cabins out here or anything?" It seemed strange that all this land would be uninhabited.

"Not in this area. The Taylor Highway isn't maintained in the winter."

"What about airports?"

"Only if you land on a lake. The terrain and weather are too extreme to get up here on anything other than a snowmobile. Even then, you don't make it that far."

Cameron looked out her side window. It was the perfect place for John to hide if he never wanted to be found. She glanced over at the sergeant, who appeared lost in his thoughts as he stared out the windshield. This was her opportunity.

"I saw that poster in the bar about that young woman who was murdered," she said. "Did you work on her case?"

"I did. I am. It's never off my mind. It's been a frustrating investigation."

"Why's that?"

"Well, to be honest, I'm not optimistic that her murder will ever be solved. Her killer was smart; left no DNA. I don't think he was someone she knew. Tok is the main junction on the Alaska Highway between the Canadian border and Fairbanks, which makes it a major stop for truckers.

"There were a ton of visitors staying in Tok for a dog sled race the night Bethany went missing. The Wolf Pack was busy. Maybe it's old-fashioned where you're from but a lot of people pay with cash up here. So, there's no way of tracking a lot of the patrons that night."

Cameron remembered the live video surveillance she'd seen on a screen mounted behind the bar. "Didn't they have surveillance cameras?"

"They had a couple of cameras rolling, but they weren't recording."

"Why not? I mean, isn't that the whole purpose of having them?"

"The bar owner thought making the live feeds visible would be enough of a deterrent. So, yeah, they were totally useless. I hate to say it, but I don't think we'll ever know who killed her."

"Sounds like her killer may have killed before," Cameron thought out loud.

Dane shot her a look as if surprised by her observation. A few minutes went by before he spoke again. "So, what do you usually shoot?"

An image of Miles's head flying backward from the gunshot filled her mind. And his blood splatter that covered her hand holding the gun. She turned to the trooper with wide eyes. "What?"

"You said you're going on a guided hunt next week. What do you usually hunt?"

"Oh." Cameron let out the air she held in her lungs. She thought about making up more lies about animals she wanted to hunt but didn't need him asking questions she couldn't answer. "This is my first time."

"Oh, wow, good for you." Dane pointed out the windshield. "There's the lake."

Cameron confirmed it on her GPS and started her descent toward the small, oval-shaped white lake. As she flew lower, she spotted two lone cabins on the northwest side of the lake. They dropped close to hover over the treetops on the south side of the lake, and Cameron felt a panic rise in her chest.

"How do you know the ice is thick enough to hold us?"

"It's plenty thick. Trust me. I've landed here in the winter with other pilots plenty of times."

Cameron stared at the snow-covered lake and fought the urge to pull back on the yoke as they descended toward the lake. "Are you sure?"

Dane chuckled through the headset. "I'm sure. The ice is at least three feet thick. You could drive a tank on it."

Cameron's heart pounded inside her chest as she brought the plane down on the snow-covered ice. The plane made impact with the frozen lake and bumped atop the surface, jumping over small snow drifts. She sagged against her seat with relief as she hit the brakes, before realizing they did nothing to slow the plane on the snow. Cameron had never felt a plane do this before. It was like being out of control on ice skates, at a hundred miles an hour. They continued toward the trees at the edge of the lake, and she stomped the left rudder in with her foot. The plane spun to the left, skidding sideways until finally it came to a stop a few feet from the bank.

Cameron's pulse still raced as she turned off the engine and removed her headset. Snow was flying everywhere. She turned to the sergeant to find him grinning at her.

"Not bad for your first landing on the ice."

"That was actually kind of fun." She smiled back and followed him out of the plane. "Once I knew we weren't going to sink."

A man headed toward them when they stepped onto the ice. A shotgun was slung over his shoulder. *Now that's a way to greet someone*, Cameron thought.

"What's with the gun?" Dane called out.

"I didn't recognize the plane."

As the older man neared them, Cameron noticed his tall build and square jaw bore a striking resemblance to the sergeant.

"What are you doing up here?" The man stopped a few feet away. His tone was gruff. He hadn't so much as looked in Cameron's direction. His dark eyes settled on Dane with disapproval.

"I came to check on you." The sergeant's tone matched that of the older man's. "You haven't answered your phone in over a week."

"I've been busy. Fishing has been good. What? You think I kicked the can or something?"

George's hairline was identical to Dane's. Cameron zipped up the neck of her down coat as the men continued to argue.

"I was worried about you."

"Well, you came all this way for nothing." Without another word, the man turned back toward the shore.

"There's a storm coming in tomorrow. You can't stay up here! I got a call from your cardiologist in Fairbanks saying you missed your appointment last month. The nurse said you're two months overdue for your follow up."

The older man continued walking without any acknowledgement of Sergeant Waska's words.

THE FINAL HUNT

The sergeant's eyes remained fixed on the old man's back. "Nice to see you too, Dad," Dane muttered under his breath.

CHAPTER TWENTY-TWO

Cameron glanced at the darkening sky after Dane's father retreated inside his cabin. They were running out of daylight if they were going to make it back to Tok tonight.

"I don't think there's any way he'll come back with us right now." Dane turned to Cameron. "I know it's a lot to ask, but would you mind if we spent the night? Maybe he'll come to his senses by morning and fly back with us before the storm comes through." He pointed to a small, A-frame structure next to the one his father had gone into. "We can stay at my cabin. I'll take the couch. And I packed some food, just in case."

"Um. Sure." Maybe she could learn more details about Bethany's murder before the night was over.

"Really?"

"Yeah."

"Thanks."

By the time Dane and Cameron secured Karl's plane to the frozen surface, it was completely dark.

"I'm sorry I brought you up here." Dane offered his hand as Cameron's foot slid on the ice.

She held onto the trooper's large palm and allowed him to steady her. Dane pulled a small flashlight from his coat pocket. They followed the light as they walked side by side.

"It's okay. I get it. He's your dad. I would feel the same way if my dad was still around."

"Oh, I'm sorry. Did you lose your dad recently?"

"Several years ago. My parents were killed in a car accident on the way to my graduation from—" she stopped, realizing she was about to say dental school. "College."

"Wow. That must've been tough."

She recalled Miles holding her in his arms when she got the news of their deadly crash. "It was."

"Losing a parent is hard. My mom passed a few years back too." Dane stared at the small cabin on the edge of the lake. A dim light filtered out through the cabin's front window. "He's the most stubborn person I've ever known. My mom was the only person he'd ever listen to. And then only rarely."

When they reached the shore, she followed Dane to the left. She guessed he was more upset about his dad than he cared to admit. She tucked her gloved hands inside her pockets and followed close beside the sergeant to keep up with the beam from his flashlight.

They trod through the snow in silence, and her thoughts drifted to John. He'd been estranged from his parents and had said they were alcoholics who refused to get help. She wondered if that was another lie. According to Mulholland,

John killed for the first time when he was a teenager. Had his parents seen signs of who he really was? Why hadn't they done something?

Dane stopped when they reached his cabin. Unlike his father's, his was unlit. Cameron gripped the frozen deck railing as she followed the trooper up the steps.

"Can you hold this?" He held the flashlight toward her when they reached the cabin's front door. "I have to find my keys."

He set his duffle bag on the ground and Cameron shined the small light on his bag as he withdrew a set of keys from the side pocket. She moved the light toward the doorknob as he unlocked the door. She followed him inside the dark cabin.

She closed the door behind her as he turned on a camping lantern. "There's no electricity up here." He grabbed a box of matches from the kitchen counter.

"Oh." Cameron watched him light a few kerosene lamps that were spread out around the room. "At all?"

He blew out the match after lighting the third lamp. "Nope."

Cameron looked around the dimly lit space. The A-frame cabin was small. The main living space was comprised of a kitchenette and small living room. The interior walls were made of the same knotted pine as her motel room and the Wolf Pack Bar. It felt only slightly warmer than outside. She shivered beneath her coat.

9

The sergeant moved toward a wood-burning stove at the edge of the room. There was a small stack of chopped wood beside it. "I'll get a fire going."

Dane placed a few pieces of kindling into the stove. She crossed the small space and sat on the flannel futon beside the fireplace. She withdrew her phone from her purse to check for new messages. She lifted the cheap phone she'd purchased when she bought her hair dye.

There was no service, but she realized it didn't matter. No one had her new number anyway.

She dropped the phone back inside her leather bag as Dane crumpled some paper and lit a match. Simon was going to be furious when he found out that she left without telling him. She could only imagine what the Seattle press were saying about her now. She wondered if Detective Mulholland already knew where she was.

She'd hoped coming up here would lead to evidence Mulholland could use to find John, but maybe this was all a mistake.

"There's only one bedroom, so you can sleep in there," Dane said.

The fire from the stove crackled, and Cameron could feel the heat almost immediately.

"I can sleep on the couch. Really, I don't mind."

"Please, I insist."

"Okay, thank you. Is that the bathroom?" Cameron pointed to one of the two doorways on the other side of the room.

"It is. But I only have running water up here in the summer. There's an outhouse out back."

Cameron looked for a sign that he was joking as he motioned toward a door to the side of the kitchenette.

"You can go out through there. Take the flashlight and you'll see it about twenty feet back."

No wonder he's so worried about his dad being up here alone. She hadn't known places this primitive still existed in the U.S. Cameron looked back at Dane before moving slowly toward the door. She did have to pee, and there was no way she could hold it until morning.

When she stepped outside, she used the beam from the flashlight to find the outhouse's roofline. It was straight back from the cabin. Her boots sank into the deep snow as she used her flashlight to scan her surroundings for wildlife. She moved quicker, thinking of what Valerie had said about rabid wolves.

She hurried up the steps when she reached the small wooden structure and shined the flashlight inside the tiny space before stepping inside. She tucked the flashlight in her coat pocket while she unzipped her jeans. The thin walls blocked the wind, making it much easier to relieve herself in the subzero temperature than she expected.

As soon as she finished, she made a dash back for the cabin. She lifted her legs up out of the snow as fast as she could, trying not to visualize the enormous wolf back at her motel.

When she opened the cabin door, Dane stood and moved toward the small cooler he'd brought sitting next to the door.

"I packed a couple sandwiches and some beer. Would you like some?"

"Sure." She crossed the room and took a seat on the futon beside the fire. "Ooh, it's warmer in here!"

Dane made a grand gesture toward the fire he had built. He brought her a sandwich in a Ziplock bag and set two beer bottles on the wood coffee table before taking a seat beside her. "Sorry it's not more." He used a bottle opener from his keychain to pop the caps.

"This is great." Cameron took a bite of her ham sandwich and discovered how hungry she was. She turned to Dane. "It's really good."

He smiled. "I live alone, and I'm not much of a cook. But I can make a mean sandwich."

"Do you think your dad will come back with us in the morning?"

Dane took another bite before answering. "Hope so. He thinks he's tough as nails, but he's too old to be up here alone in the winter. It drives me crazy."

"You know…" Dane broke the silence after finishing his sandwich. "You asked earlier about Bethany, and I didn't mention what a great person she was. After her body was found, the media completely focused on her killer. And that we hadn't caught him. The fact that she was a human being, and a wonderful one, was completely overlooked. She deserves to be remembered as more than an unsolved murder victim."

"Can you tell me about her?" Cameron turned to face him. Her leg brushed against his when she adjusted her position on the small futon. If he noticed, he didn't show it.

"She was caring. Put others before herself. She'd gotten a full ride to the University of Washington. But after she moved away for her first year of college, her younger sister fell into a deep depression. She's four years younger than Bethany, and she really struggled after Bethany moved away. In Alaska, we have the highest suicide rate in the country. Tok has long dark winters. And being a small town, Bethany's sister didn't have many friends.

"So, Bethany gave up her scholarship and moved back to Tok after her freshman year at UW. She took out a loan to get her teaching degree online from the University of Alaska. She was working at the Wolf Pack to help pay for school.

"Her body was found in the woods six days after she went missing. The frozen temperature slowed down her decomposition. She was dehydrated and likely kept alive by her captor for two or three days before she was killed. There were ligature marks on her wrists from being bound, and she'd been raped—multiple times." His voice wavered and he broke Cameron's gaze to stare straight ahead at the small window facing the lake, even though there was nothing to see but darkness.

None of John's other victims had been bound. But after John had been scratched by his last victim, which was how Mulholland was able to prove his guilt, he would know to be more careful. Especially now, when his calculated escape plan could fall apart. Bethany was also kept alive longer than John's previous victims.

Her sandwich rose to the top of her throat. Cameron swallowed it back down, trying to temper her revulsion in front of the state trooper. *He'd been taking his time. Savoring it.*

Dane's voice interrupted her thoughts. "Initially, we thought Bethany's murder might've been connected to a woman who was killed while visiting Tok a year ago. But that tourist's murder was just solved, and her killer was working in Washington State at the time of Bethany's death."

Cameron choked on her beer. *That's because John killed Bethany.*

"I hate seeing her family around town knowing Bethany's case will likely never be solved. She didn't deserve to die."

Dane brushed his cheek on the far side of his face with the back of his hand. Cameron watched him, wondering if he was crying. But he cleared his throat and stood from the futon before she could get a better look.

"I'm tired. I bet you are, too." Dane moved toward the door on the far-left side of the living room. "I'm gonna grab some blankets for the couch." Please help yourself to anything. There's more food in the cooler."

"Thanks." Cameron took a sip from her beer as Dane disappeared inside the bedroom, carrying a kerosene lamp.

He returned a moment later with a wool blanket and a pillow in his arms. Their eyes locked when he set the bedding on the futon next to Cameron.

"Well, I better let you get some rest." She stood from the futon.

"I have a shirt you can wear to sleep in if you want."

"Oh. Okay." She returned his awkward smile before heading toward the bedroom, which was dimly lit from the kerosene lamp Dane had left on the dresser.

The room felt cooler than the living room. A flannel button-up shirt was laid out atop the bed. The sergeant was tall, over six feet. Cameron could tell just by looking that the shirt would be almost to her knees. She placed her hand on the soft, worn-in fabric. Despite the strangeness of sleeping in the sergeant's shirt, it would be more comfortable than her jeans.

She glanced at her cashmere sweater. Except for all the snow gear, she was traveling light underneath. *I can't afford for this to get balled up from sleeping in it.*

"We'll want to head back as soon as it's light out tomorrow, so we miss the storm."

Cameron jumped at the sound of Dane's voice from the doorway.

"Sorry. I didn't mean to startle you."

Cameron looked up at him, embarrassed for being so jumpy. His uniform was unbuttoned, exposing a fitted white v-neck t-shirt underneath.

"No, you didn't," she lied. "It's fine."

"If you leave the door open, your room will stay warmer tonight."

She nodded. "My cabin's the same way." She cringed. *My cabin.*

Dane started to turn away from the doorway before looking back. "And Shay?"

"Yeah?"

"Thank you for bringing me up here. My dad shouldn't stay here through this storm. I...um...really appreciate it."

"No problem."

Dane retreated to the living room and Cameron shut the door to change out of her clothes. When she pulled the oversized flannel shirt over her head, she recognized the scent of the sergeant's aftershave. She perched on the edge of the bed and looked around the small room, thinking of what Dane said about Bethany.

Dane's words replayed in her mind: *Bethany didn't deserve to die.*

And John didn't deserve to live.

How would she find him in this vast and extreme wilderness? But another worry gnawed at her. If she led the police to John, she had no doubt John would turn her in for what she did to Miles.

Knowing John, she guessed that he had made copies of that convenience store footage. Mulholland already suspected her of killing her first husband. If John confirmed it, Mulholland would probably think she helped John too. Why wouldn't he?

Cameron opened the bedroom door; the main room was dark aside from the crackling fire. She blew out the kerosene lamp, noting the similarities between the wooden bed frame and the one at her cabin. She pulled back the sheets and slid beneath the thick layers of blankets.

The couch creaked under Dane's weight on the other side of the wall. She thought of the tears in his eyes when he spoke of Bethany. How had she managed to marry such monsters when there were men out there like Dane?

Cameron turned onto her side. She couldn't let John get away with all of this. But was she willing to sacrifice her freedom in exchange for John's?

CHAPTER TWENTY-THREE

Cameron woke to darkness and the smell of coffee. A faint light filtered into her room from the main living space. She felt as though she'd just fallen asleep. Her eyes adjusted to the dim light, and she recognized the wood log walls.

She remembered the crime photos. The dead woman. John standing over her. Admiring his kill.

Cameron propped herself up on one elbow. Why had she come back here?

She strained to make out the pattern on the quilted blanket and saw her clothes in a pile on the floor. A tall, broad figure appeared in her doorway, pushing the door open.

She shot up in bed, grasping the quilt and pulling it toward her chest. Her eyes darted around the small room in search of something she could use as a weapon. The figure took a step toward her. Cameron opened her mouth to scream as the man lifted a kerosene lamp in front of his chest.

"Don't!" She threw her hand out to protect herself.

"Shay?"

In the glowing light, Cameron recognized Sergeant Waska. He wore a white t-shirt and held a steaming coffee mug in his other hand.

"Whoa," he said. "Shay, it's me."

Cameron brought a hand to her forehead and sank against the headboard with relief. Dane stared at her with wide-eyed concern.

"Sorry," she said. "I…um…forgot where I was for a second."

He furrowed his brow as if unsure whether to believe her. "You okay?"

"Yeah." She forced a smile. "Fine. Sorry."

"I brought you some coffee."

He stepped forward cautiously. She tried to control the tremble in her hands when she accepted the steaming mug.

The state trooper took a step back toward the door, giving her space. "We need to leave soon. I convinced my dad to come with us. The snowstorm is set to reach here in about an hour."

Cameron sipped the strong coffee even though she already felt wide awake from the adrenaline pumping through her body. "Okay. What time is it?"

"It's almost eight-thirty."

Cameron lifted her head to the window above the bed. There was no light coming through the thin curtains. "It's still dark out."

He smiled. "Yeah. It won't get light for another twenty minutes. Welcome to winter in Alaska." He turned for the door. "We should be ready to leave as soon as we can."

Large sticky snowflakes blew against the windshield of Karl's plane.

"Can you help me keep an eye out for other planes?" Cameron had never flown when it was snowing, and she didn't like the waning visibility. She remembered John saying once that Alaska had the most deaths from small aircraft in the country, because they had the highest number of pilots and aircraft per capita in the world, coupled with ever-changing weather and hostile terrain.

"Sure." Dane sat up straighter in his seat beside her.

Cameron could barely make out the chunks of ice that floated atop the murky river below them, marking the halfway point back to Tok. The visibility had been much better when she'd taken off from the lake.

"How come there aren't any other cabins on that lake?" Cameron asked him through the mouthpiece to her headset. "You guys don't own the whole thing, do you?"

Dane's dad sat behind them. He'd climbed into the backseat that morning without a word. He'd uttered a single grunt since they took off.

"The land surrounding the lake is all owned by the state now," Dane said. "Those cabins belonged to my grandfather—my mom's dad—before it became state land. We can't ever sell them, but we can keep them in the family for as long as we want."

"Interesting." Cameron thought of John's life insurance money that he cashed out. As far as she knew, he had no family connections in Alaska. "I read somewhere that Alaska has different land sales laws than the rest of the country. Is it easier to buy land here?"

"You're probably thinking of over-the-counter land sales, which is a streamlined process to purchase property in Alaska. Most of it is just done online now."

"Is there a way to search for sales by the name of the purchaser?"

"Yeah, it'd be public information. Why? Are you falling in love?"

She glanced sideways at him, caught off guard by the question. "Love?"

"Yeah. A lot of people want to buy land up here after they discover the beauty and seclusion of this place."

"Oh." She felt heat rush to her cheeks. "I guess maybe I am."

"Hey, when we get back, could I buy you a drink later at the Wolf Pack? I get off around four. I owe you one."

"Sure." Maybe she could tell him the truth and ask him to help her find John. Dane seemed more trusting of her than Mulholland. But that was only because he didn't know who she really was.

"Man, this damn toothache just keeps getting worse," George spoke into his headset for this first time since they'd taken off. "Can feel it all the way up the side of my head."

"How long has it been bothering you?" Cameron asked.

George sighed loudly into the mouthpiece. "I dunno. A week. Maybe two."

"Have you noticed any swollen spots on your gums?"

"Ah…yeah, I did, yesterday. It hurts like hell."

"You could have an abscess. If it's not treated the infection could spread to your bloodstream." She glanced at Dane. "Is there a dentist in Tok?"

"Yeah." He looked back at his dad. "For another week at least. He's retiring and moving to Belize."

Cameron eyed George in the backseat over her shoulder. "You need to see him—*today*. If you don't, it could be really serious."

Dane gave her an inquisitive look. "You a dentist or something?"

"Oh." She flushed, remembering what she'd told the others in town. "No, I'm an accountant."

"For Sovas," she added. As if being more specific would add legitimacy to her lie.

"You seem to know a bit about teeth."

"Um, yeah, my ex-husband was a dentist."

They flew into a fog bank and Cameron could barely see through the thick cloud of white that surrounded the plane. She pulled back the power and started a descent to 3,000 feet, hoping the lower altitude would improve their visibility.

"Anchorage Center, Maule three-seven-four-eight November," she said into the mouthpiece of her headset.

"Maule three-seven-four-eight November, Anchorage Center," a male voice crackled through her headset.

"Maule three-seven-four-eight November, I'm twenty miles northwest of Tok Junction. Landing Tok Junction. Request flight following."

"Maule three-seven-four-eight November, you are on radar contact nineteen miles northwest of Tok Junction. You have traffic, a Piper Tri-Pacer, who reported outbound from Tok Junction about ten minutes ago heading to Delta Junction, but I don't have them on radar."

"Roger. We are descending to 3,000 feet." Cameron leaned forward and scanned the sky. "My visibility is really poor. I can't see very far ahead."

"Tri-Pacer nine-five-eight-one Bravo, what's your altitude and position?"

"Tri-Pacer nine-five-eight-one Bravo," a different male voice came through her headset. "I'm flying at three—"

"Watch out!" Dane yelled from the seat beside her. "I see them!" He pointed out the windshield.

The fog lifted as their borrowed plane continued to descend. Cameron's breath caught in her throat. A white plane flew straight toward them, less than fifty yards away.

The Tri-Pacer dipped to the side as Cameron tilted the yoke to the left. The Maule dove to the side, causing Dane to lean against her. Dane's dad swore into the headset from the backseat.

The white plane swerved in the opposite direction but remained in Cameron's path. She held her breath, jamming the yoke as far left as it would go. She could see the other pilot's terrified face as they met. In the next second, the two planes passed, their wings missing each other by mere inches.

Slowly, Cameron righted the plane as she gaped out the windshield. She felt Dane's hand on her knee.

"You did good," he said.

"We almost died," she said, keeping her eyes trained on the surrounding skies.

"I know, But we're okay."

She brought her hand to her mouth.

"Maule three-seven-four-eight November, what's your status?"

"Um." She cleared her throat.

Dane removed his hand from her knee.

"Maule three-seven-four-eight November," Cameron said, aware of her voice shaking. "We had a near miss with the white Tri-Pacer. But we are okay. Requesting permission to go to advisory frequency."

"Roger, radar service is terminated. Cleared to advisory frequency."

Dane's father placed his hand on Dane's shoulder from the backseat. Cameron figured their near-death experience prompted the sentimental gesture. Until his gruff voice came over their headsets.

"I think I would've been safer stayin' back at my cabin. Just sayin'."

CHAPTER TWENTY-FOUR

Cameron dug inside her purse for her motel key after Dane dropped her off. She climbed the two steps of her miniature cabin's porch. The white vapor from her breath lingered in the air as she unlocked the door. She flipped on the lights before stepping inside. After plugging in her phone, she stripped off her clothes.

She stepped under the bathroom's tiny shower head. The warm water turned a pale orange around her feet after running through her hair from her recent dye job. She closed her eyes and breathed in the steam, trying to remember what life was like before all of this.

But her mind kept returning to John's crime photos. And what Dane had said about Bethany. Cameron was certain that John had killed her. She found herself shivering and realized the water had run cold. She stepped out of the shower and dried herself with the thin, rough towel that hung on the wall.

When she caught her reflection in the bathroom mirror, she hardly recognized herself. But the color suited her. If she didn't know better, it could look natural.

She dressed in the warmest clothes she'd packed, wishing she'd come more prepared for the subzero temperatures. She slid her laptop from her bag and opened it atop the tiny desk against the wall. If John had used his life insurance payout to purchase property in the area, he could be in police custody tonight.

Although it wouldn't give back the lives he'd taken, and her life would still be forever marred by his crimes.

Cameron ran an Internet search for property sales records in Alaska and found the webpage for the Alaska Department of Natural Resources. She clicked through the website until she found a place to search for Alaska property purchases going back to 2001. She typed John's name into the search bar and selected Southeast Fairbanks County.

A list of results came up, all starting with John, but with different last names. She scrolled through the list. No John Prescott. She widened the search to the entire state. A longer list of Johns with different last names filled her screen. She went through the names again before closing her laptop. *Of course John hadn't purchased property up here in his own name.*

Then she remembered what Dane had said about inheriting their lake cabins. John didn't have any family connections in Alaska, but Miles did. His grandfather had a cabin somewhere in the remote wilderness. Miles's parents hadn't wanted it, so his grandfather left it to him. Miles had only spoken of it once, when they were dating. He said he hadn't been up there since he was a kid.

If John knew about what she'd done to Miles, maybe he also knew about the cabin.

She reopened her laptop and typed Miles's name in the same search bar she'd searched for John's. It yielded no results. But Miles didn't buy the property, he inherited it.

She called the number listed on the website. A woman answered after the second ring.

"Department of Natural Resources, how can I help you?"

"Hi. I'm trying to find a record of ownership for a private property that was inherited about fifteen years ago. Is there somewhere I can search online for that?"

"Inherited.... If the property was inherited, you'll have to fill out an online records request with the Recorder's Office for the area you're searching for."

"And will that give me a list of names of property owners?"

"Yes. Do you have the property address?"

"Um. No."

"Do you know the area where the property is located?"

Cameron racked her brain, trying to recall everything Miles had said about it. "It's in a remote area. I think in the Charley Rivers area."

"You probably want to search near the Yukon-Charley Rivers National Preserve then. That's remote all right. Won't be many private properties around there."

"Can you run the search for me now?"

"I'm sorry, no. You'll have to fill out the request online with the recorder's office. Then you should get an email with results within ten business days."

"*Ten days?*" Mulholland could have her arrested before then. "I really need this information. Is there any way to get it sooner? Please."

There was a pause before the woman answered. "Well, I can make a call and ask them to expedite your results. And you can make a note of that in your request. But it will probably depend on who you get."

"Thank you. Yes, please call them for me. And I'll fill out that form right now."

Cameron submitted the online form as soon as she hung up. *Ten days for the results?* Her stomach growled, and she figured she might as well eat. There wasn't much more she could do but wait.

She sighed as she pulled on her coat. She stopped in her tracks a few feet from the door and stared up at the enormous stuffed wolf.

The sheet she'd thrown over it yesterday was gone. Cameron turned and saw it neatly folded atop the bed. She looked back at the large beast. Her eyes rested on a small white paper folded between its teeth. She crept toward it and snatched the paper from its jaw.

She sank atop the spring mattress after unfolding the note. Three words were handwritten in red ink under the Howling Wolf Motel letterhead: *GO HOME CAMERON.*

CHAPTER TWENTY-FIVE

Cameron stared at the neatly penned block letters. No one in Tok knew her as Cameron. She looked around the room. The deadbolt was still locked.

Was John watching her? Was she getting close to him?

She studied the tall, blocky letters that appeared to have been scribbled in haste. It wasn't John's handwriting. Who else would leave the note? Detective Mulholland? She brushed the thought aside. If he wanted her to come back, he wouldn't leave her some creepy note. Surely, that's not how he operated. But then who? No one knew she was here.

She hadn't even told Simon. He would be livid when he discovered she'd left without telling him—or the police. She opened her laptop and logged into her email. Simon didn't have her new number, but he would try to communicate with her however he could.

She chewed her lip as she waited for her inbox to load. People did not come to this place for the Internet speed. There it was. Three unread messages from Simon. She cringed when she read the subject lines, which increased in intensity with each one he'd sent.

Where are you?

Call me!!

Let me know you're ok! Where the hell are you?!

Cameron didn't need to open the emails to know what they said. Instead, she looked up his phone number on the website for his law firm. He answered on the second ring.

"Simon Castelli." His words came out in a rush.

"It's me. Cameron."

"Cam! Are you okay?"

"I'm fine. I—"

"Where the hell are you?" Anger replaced his relief.

"I—"

"I didn't even know if you were alive! I thought—I've been so worried. The media have been speculating that you're suicidal."

Cameron winced at the word. The moment of ending it all when she flew over John's cabin came back. But how would the media know that?

"You can't just up and leave with all this going on. Don't you know how it looks? Not just to the media, but the police."

"I'm sorry, Simon. I am."

"I'm doing all I can for you, but you're not making it easy."

"I just couldn't take it anymore. Being in that house. What the reporters were saying."

"I could've helped you with that. Where are you?"

"I'm in Tok."

"Where?"

"Alaska."

"Why the hell are you in Alaska?"

He wasn't going to like her answer. "I just need to make sure John didn't get away with all this. I need answers, Simon."

She heard him breathe into the phone. She knew how crazy she sounded.

"Why Alaska?"

She sank against the cheap wooden chair, grateful he kept his reprimands to himself. "A hunch. A gut feeling. It seems like exactly the kind of place John would want to escape to. I know it sounds crazy."

"You've been through a lot. I'm concerned about you. And you being up there alone. That doesn't sound like a safe place for a woman like yourself."

Like herself? Did he forget she shared a bed with a violent serial murderer *and* rapist for the last decade? What could be less safe than that?

"Just come home, Cameron. I'll help sort everything out. Did you hear what I said? The press is speculating that you're suicidal and the police are looking at you as an accomplice. And by running up to Alaska, you're only fueling their allegations."

Cameron looked down at the note still in her hand. She decided not to tell him. It would only add to his fury.

"The police know you took your plane, and if you've got it parked at an airport up there, it won't be long until they find out where you are. They don't have enough to arrest you—"

"I haven't done anything!"

"I know. But listen. I saw the traffic camera footage of your car on I-90 the night those teachers went missing. Mulholland wasn't lying. It was definitely your Lexus."

She never went to the cabin without John before his disappearance. And she had no recollection of driving over the mountain pass that summer. She had no reason to.

"Could you see who was driving?"

"No. It's basically a weather camera for the pass. But my point is that your running off like this won't look good to a jury—if it comes to that."

Cameron stiffened. "What are you saying? That I'm going to be arrested for helping John because my car was on I-90? Last I checked that's not a crime. I thought you were a better lawyer than that."

She regretted the bitter words as soon as they left her tongue. They were met with silence, making her feel even worse. She leaned her elbow onto the desk and cradled her face in her palm. "Why do I feel like I'm the one who's being tried for John's crimes?"

"You're not. And I'm trying to make sure you won't be. Come back, and I'll help you sort all this out."

I can't. Not until I find him. "I'll come back soon. I promise."

"Cam—"

She ended the call and put her other hand up to her face. How can this be happening? How could Mulholland really think she had anything to do with this? Could she really be charged with being an accessory to John? The traffic camera footage can't be enough to charge her with being an accomplice to *murder*. Not in these times with modern forensic evidence. Didn't the police need more than that? But then why did Simon mention how it would look to a jury?

Cameron stood. Bethany had disappeared after her shift at the Wolf Pack Bar, which made it the one place in this town she was certain John had been. Someone had to remember something.

She had come in search of John to find answers. But finding him wouldn't exonerate her—not to the police. Killing him, however, would be justice. Even if it came at the cost of her own freedom.

Her stomach growled. She hadn't eaten anything since the eggs Dane had made her for breakfast. She wasn't meeting him at the bar for a few more hours, but she might as well go now and get some food in her stomach. Try to find out more about the night Bethany went missing. Cameron went into the tiny bathroom to check her reflection before leaving. Her short hair was nearly dry.

She thought of the trooper last night at his cabin. How he broke down talking about Bethany. And his concern for his father.

Despite her troubles, she smiled at the apples he kept in his SUV and how he defied the cliché of the donut-eating cop. She turned from the mirror to retrieve her makeup bag. A little mascara and lipstick couldn't hurt.

CHAPTER TWENTY-SIX

Tanner sat alone in the squared-off cubicle reserved for his squad. But he was used to it. Even preferred it. He worked better in the quiet. When the rest of his squad clocked out to pick up their kids and have dinner with their families, he stayed.

He finished reading through Miles Henson's autopsy report for the second time. The coroner had determined the manner of death a suicide caused by severe craniocerebral trauma from a gunshot wound to the head. The trajectory and close range of the shot was consistent with being self-inflicted. The house had burned for a while before the fire department was able to retrieve Miles's body, leaving his remains severely charred.

Tanner reached into his jacket pocket then remembered he'd used his last stick of gum hours ago. After learning Cameron's Cessna was missing from her Renton Airport hangar, he'd put out a request and locate bulletin for her plane. That afternoon, he'd gotten a call from an Alaska State

Trooper informing him that her plane was parked at an airport in Tok, Alaska.

He didn't have enough evidence to arrest Cameron for being John's accomplice, but at least now he could keep tabs on her whereabouts. To go up there, she must really be convinced John was alive. But that didn't necessarily prove her innocence.

If she *had* been helping John, she might've questioned the bear attack. If she thought John had left her out of his escape plan, she could have brought the crime scene photos in out of revenge. And when she learned that Tanner already suspected John, it would have sparked her rage and solidified her belief that John faked his death.

But she probably hadn't counted on herself becoming a suspect in return.

"You work too hard, Mulholland!" One of the detectives hollered on their way out.

Tanner rubbed his strained eyes before scrolling up a page on Miles's autopsy report. Miles's lungs showed no evidence of smoke inhalation. Even though he started the fire before pulling the trigger. The gunshot was determined to be instantly fatal, so it was possible Miles started the fire right before killing himself.

Or, someone else started the fire after he was shot.

Tanner looked back at the photo of Miles's charred body inside his home. He was found slumped over on his living room couch, with his hand tucked against his waist and his pistol still in his grip. Tanner studied the angle of Miles's body. While it was likely impossible to prove Miles didn't naturally end up in that position, it struck him as unusual the gun didn't slip from his grip.

Tanner shut off his computer after the last detective from the evening squad told him good night on her way out.

"Goodnight, Richards."

Tanner stretched his arms above his head, glad he ran five miles that morning before coming in. Because now it was time to get some sleep.

Alicia Lopez's missing persons file remained open on his desk. He closed it and stood halfway up before he opened it again. He flipped back to the page containing the dental records that were included with the initial report. He scanned the page to the bottom for the name of the dentist that released them.

He read it again to make sure he wasn't seeing things. Maybe he *had* worked too long. But beneath the dentist's signature was a clearly printed name.

He opened the missing persons file underneath it for Olivia Rossi, the other teacher found at Prescott's cabin. He flicked through the pages until he found the dental records. The dental records had been released by the same dentist as Alicia Lopez: Dr. Cameron Prescott.

CHAPTER TWENTY-SEVEN

Willie Nelson's greatest hits played from the jukebox as Cameron sat beside an already drunk Karl. She took a sip from her second iced tea. Other than Joan, they were the only two in the bar on this weekday afternoon. She checked her watch. It was just before four. Dane would be arriving any minute.

Karl broke into song, belting out the country lyrics off-tune. He rocked atop his barstool as he sang, and Cameron was afraid he was going to take a fall onto the wood floor. She watched with amazement as he stayed upright.

She moved her attention to Joan. Even though she wasn't working that night Bethany went missing, Joan still could have seen John around town. But, in the hours she'd sat at the bar, Cameron didn't know how to ask her without Joan wondering why she was questioning whether The Teacher Killer was in Tok after his supposed death.

Joan was focused on the news that played on the small TV in the corner of the bar. The bartender grabbed the remote off the counter and turned up the volume so it could be heard over Karl's obnoxious singing.

Cameron took another drink and followed Joan's gaze to the TV. She choked on the cold liquid when she saw her own face in the corner of the screen.

Joan turned toward her. "Are you okay?"

Cameron nodded, forcing herself to look away from the breaking news story long enough to assure Joan she was fine. "Just went down the wrong pipe."

Both women returned their attention to the news. Karl sang louder and it took all of Cameron's self-control to refrain from shouting at him to shut up. Thankfully, Joan turned up the volume again.

"New evidence has emerged involving Dr. Cameron Prescott, wife of the late John Prescott, whose crimes award him the nickname, The Teacher Killer."

Cameron darted her eyes toward Joan and Karl, but their attentions were fixed on the screen. Would they recognize her? Cameron returned her focus to the TV. In the photo they displayed, Cameron had long blonde hair and full makeup. It was the professional headshot she used for her dental practice. Cameron could only hope she'd done a good enough job altering her appearance as the dark-haired reporter continued.

"Dr. Prescott hasn't been seen in the three days since she left her Laurelhurst home without telling the police. Police confirm that her Cessna is missing from its Renton Airport hangar and suspect she's hiding out in a remote location. While initial reports speculated the killer's wife was suicidal, police have just released new information that may link the Laurelhurst dentist to her late husband's crimes."

Cameron thought of the credit card she'd given Valerie when she checked in. Would she recognize her name from the news? Would someone recognize her Cessna?

Cameron felt a cold blast of air as the door to the bar opened, but she didn't turn around. She strained to hear what the reporter was saying as Joan turned down the volume.

"The usual?" Joan called out.

"Yeah, thanks," a man said.

Cameron glanced over her shoulder to see a couple with a teenage girl. Their faces were void of expression as they took seats around a booth. Cameron turned back to the TV. The reporter's voice was now drowned out by Lyle Lovett's high-pitched, nasal lyrics. Karl hummed along at the barstool beside her.

Cameron expected to see the traffic camera footage of her Lexus on I-90, but instead an image of her dental practice filled the screen. She eyed the remote at the end of the bar, desperate to hear the rest of what the reporter was saying. But she didn't dare draw attention to the news story about herself.

Joan carried a tray with two beers and a Coke to the family at the booth. If she'd recognized Cameron from the news, she had an excellent poker face. The news finally cut from the exterior of her dental office and returned to the pretty reporter's somber face before going to a commercial.

Joan returned with an empty tray and leaned against the bar on the other side of Cameron. Cameron felt a ripple of fear when the bartender's eyes met hers. Had she recognized her? Was she going to turn her in?

Cameron tried to think of what she would say when Joan accused her of being John Prescott's wife when the bartender tilted her head in the direction of the family in the booth. "That's Bethany's parents. And sister, Grace."

Cameron turned around. The three of them sat in silence with their drinks untouched. She could see it now. She'd been too preoccupied to notice when they first walked in, but there was no mistaking the sadness written all over their faces.

She recognized Bethany's parents from an online photo, but Bethany's younger sister was practically unrecognizable from the buoyant young girl Cameron had seen in the family photo taken before Bethany's death.

Cameron turned back around, not wanting to stare. She was struck by how obviously ravaged Grace was by her older sister's death. The dark circles under her eyes were a stark contrast to her pale face. And even with her winter layers, Cameron thought she looked unhealthily skinny.

"Do they come here often?" she asked Joan.

Joan nodded. "If it were me, I'd never want to step foot in this bar again. But I think they feel close to her here."

Cameron took another drink from her iced tea. She longed to hug them, tell them how sorry she was for what John did. For her part in not recognizing him for who he really was. But there was nothing that would ever give them back what John had taken from them.

Joan moved down the bar to get Karl another beer when Cameron's phone rang. It had to be either Simon or Dane. They were the only ones with her number.

She fumbled inside her purse until her fingers closed around her phone. She held it up, glad to see the 907 area code.

"Hi."

"Cameron, hey. It's Dane." An engine revved in the background. "I'm afraid I'll have to take a rain check on that drink."

"Oh. Okay." She tried to hide the disappointment in her voice.

"I just got a call that an inmate up in Fairbanks confessed to killing Bethany. I'm heading there now."

Cameron glanced at Bethany's family across the bar. "An inmate?" *Could it be John?* She quickly dismissed the thought. If John was arrested, they would have fingerprinted him and discovered who he really was.

"He was sentenced to twenty-five years earlier this month for armed robbery. He's going to be transferred to Spring Creek tomorrow. It's a maximum-security prison in Seward."

"Do you think he's telling the truth?"

"I don't know. I'm hoping to find out when I interview him. There were details from Bethany's murder we never released to the public. Anyway, I'll let you know when I'm back in town."

That inmate didn't kill Bethany. John did. But how would she ever convince anyone if another man was charged with her killing?

Dane was smart. He would figure out that prisoner was lying. *Right?*

A female voice came through the call, echoing from Dane's police scanner.

"And Shay?"

The sound of being someone else felt good. "Yeah?"

"My dad went to the dentist earlier, and the doc said it was the worst abscess he'd ever seen. He said if he'd waited much longer, it could've spread to his bloodstream like you warned. So, thanks for telling him he should go. If I had told him, he never would have listened."

"Glad to hear it. Drive safe."

Cameron stood from the bar after leaving a tip for Joan. She stole one last look at Bethany's family, who continued to sit in silence with their barely touched drinks. Bethany's sister looked up when Cameron opened the door.

The girl looked down at her lap as Cameron left the Wolf Pack. A gust of sub-zero wind accosted her like a slap in the face as Cameron started toward her motel along the inside of a snowbank beside the two-lane highway.

Of Bethany's family, her younger sister seemed the most tragic to Cameron. She was so young; had her whole life ahead of her. And yet she was so obviously ravaged by her sister's death.

Dusk settled over the town during her frigid walk back to her motel. She passed the Tok Visitor Center, which was surrounded by an empty, snow-blanketed parking lot. A large sign on the log cabin's front window read *CLOSED FOR THE SEASON*. Streaks of orange peaked through the clouds when Cameron climbed the steps to the motel's front office.

Her legs felt numb from the cold beneath her jeans. Glad to see the lights were still on, Cameron stomped the snow off her boots before she pulled open the heavy door and stepped inside. Valerie was reclined with her boots atop the desk. Her ankles were crossed, and her face was hidden behind a paperback novel. The Fairbanks news played on a small tube TV behind Valerie's head. The volume was turned down, but Cameron was glad to see the newscaster was no longer talking about her. Not that Valerie paid any attention to it anyway.

Instead of greeting her, the manager turned a page. As Cameron neared the desk, she recognized the bestselling crime thriller that captivated the woman's attention. The book was set in Seattle. Cameron used to love reading crime novels.

"What can I do for you, dear?" Valerie's gaze followed her novel as she set it aside.

"I'm staying in Cabin A and—"

"I know."

"Right. Anyway, I was wondering who has access to my room. I locked the door before leaving yesterday and when I got back this morning around eleven, it seemed someone had been in my room."

The woman looked genuinely surprised. "What do you mean? Was something missing?"

"No. Nothing was missing. It…um…just wasn't exactly how I'd left it. Do you happen to know if someone went in my room while I was gone?"

"What exactly was different?"

Cameron bit the inside of her lip. She wasn't about to tell this woman about the note, but she was beyond worrying about offending her. "I'd placed a sheet over the wolf and when I got back it had been removed."

The manager pulled her feet off the counter and sat up straight. "You don't like the wolf?"

"Did you see anyone come to the motel yesterday or early this morning?"

"No." The older woman's mouth crept into a cryptic smile. "Maybe the wolf did it. While you were out. You probably hurt her feelings."

Cameron pursed her lips together. This was useless. Over Valerie's shoulder, a male newscaster appeared on the screen, and Cameron's photo appeared in the upper right corner. She strained to hear what he was saying as he started off the five o'clock news hour with the same breaking news story that had played at the bar.

Valerie turned to see what had captivated Cameron's attention. An image of John filled the screen. *THE TEACHER KILLER* appeared in bold letters beneath his photo as the reporter continued in a volume too low for Cameron to hear.

Valerie turned back to her. "Mauled by a bear, right? Lucky son of a bitch if you ask me. That's an easy way to go. Guy like that should've been attacked by wolves. *That* would've been justice."

Cameron tore her eyes from the TV. What difference was there in being killed by a bear or a wolf? Both seemed equally brutal ways to go. She needed to get back to her room and find out what the reporter was saying, but curiosity got the better of her.

"What do you mean?"

Valerie's eyes lit up as if Cameron had just told her she'd won the lottery. She leaned her elbows onto the desk. "Unlike bears, or the big cats, wolves eat their prey alive. When they attack humans, which does occur in cases of rabid wolves and rogue packs of juvenile males, it's a harrowing death. Bears tend to go straight for the head or neck, killing their prey almost instantly." Her eyes moved to the white wolf behind Cameron. "But wolves hunt down their prey in a pack. They surround their victims and disarm them slowly with excruciating, non-fatal blows until their victim finally collapses from exhaustion—and pain. They bite and gnash at the hindquarters, hamstringing their prey to take out the hind legs. The wolves will then start to devour their prey immediately, starting with the gut and the groin, so their victims will often stay alive for quite some time." She lowered her eyes from the wolf and met Cameron's. "Can't imagine a worse way to go than that. Can you?"

Cameron shook her head, wishing she didn't have to sleep in the same room with one tonight. Stuffed or not.

"Sorry, dear. I hope I haven't scared you. If you *do* come upon a wolf, always maintain eye contact. It will keep them at bay." She chuckled. "Well, unless they have rabies. Then it won't matter—you'll just have to shoot them."

Cameron took a step back. "Thanks for your time."

"You're welcome, sweetheart. Oh. I almost forgot." Valerie reached behind the desk. "I thought you might want to borrow this." She set a faded paperback book on the counter with a photo of a large white wolf on the cover. Just like the ones in the motel. "You might find this interesting before you go on your trapping trip." She pushed the book toward Cameron. "There's no greater thrill than hunting down an apex predator such as the wolf."

Cameron stared at the book before picking it up, thinking of John.

"I know you said you're hoping to trap a lynx, but after reading this, you might change your mind."

"Thanks," Cameron said. "I'll bring this back when I'm done."

The sky was dark when Cameron walked around the side of the lodge toward her cabin. After unlocking the door to her room, she flicked on the lights. The stuffed wolf gave her a start, making her feel paranoid as she sank onto the bed. It wasn't like she hadn't known it was there.

She made a cup of tea in the small kitchenette and turned off the lights before sitting down at the desk. After everything she'd learned about wolves, she couldn't stand looking at the beast any longer. Or feeling like it was watching *her*.

She sipped her Earl Grey in the glow from her laptop and typed her name into the Internet search bar. Several headlines with today's date filled the results. She set down her mug, sloshing hot liquid onto her hand when she read the top result.

BOTH WOMEN FOUND BURIED AT PRESCOTT'S CABIN PATIENTS OF HIS WIFE'S DENTAL PRACTICE

Her jaw dropped. She clicked on the bold headline, the mounted wolf now gone from her mind. Her thoughts whirled as she read the article. Technically, they were both her patients. Her front office manager had sent their records to the police after they were reported missing. It was standard procedure, and they weren't the first of her patients to ever require dental records for identification.

At the time, she'd barely recalled one of the women and hadn't remembered the other. One of them hadn't been into her office in over a year. The other had only been in once. They weren't labeled as victims of The Teacher Killer, since all his previous victims had been found alone in their homes.

But it didn't look good. She slammed her laptop closed and sat in the dark. Had John picked her patients on purpose?

If Mulholland suspected her before, what must he be thinking now? None of John's other victims had been patients of her office, but the article didn't mention that. Her phone rang, making her jump.

She checked the caller ID. *Simon.* Not having the emotional energy to explain herself, she pressed *Ignore.*

Maybe coming here was a mistake. If that inmate really had killed Bethany, then all she was doing was making herself look guilty by skipping town. Had she allowed herself to believe John was still alive so she wouldn't have to face reality?

She should go back home and talk to Mulholland. Tell him she didn't know those two teachers even though they were technically her patients. That she came up here based on her wild theory that John was still alive and hiding out somewhere in Alaska.

In the darkness, she pondered John knowing what she'd done to Miles. She lifted her laptop screen and checked her email. Her heart jumped when she saw the email from the recorder's office with the subject line: *List of private property owners in Yukon-Charley Rivers.*

Her phone chimed with a voicemail notification. But she didn't take her eyes off the screen.

She opened the email and held her breath as she read through the short list of names. She stopped halfway through the results. Andrew Henson was listed beside a property address. *Miles's grandfather.* Miles must have never transferred it into his name. She opened the map that was attached to the email and located the property. It was in the middle of a mountainous wilderness area in Northeast Alaska, about one hundred miles from Eagle, where Valerie had shot that record wolf.

Her body went still as she stared at the map. She'd been right. He was hiding out there. He had to be.

All these years, John had known her darkest secret. The thing that had consumed her with guilt and fear. And he planned to use it against her.

For such a careful planner, John had made a critical mistake. How could he have been so stupid to betray her when he'd known what she'd done?

THE FINAL HUNT

She hadn't killed her first husband only to be destroyed by her second.

CHAPTER TWENTY-EIGHT

Snow crunched under her boots as Cameron listened to Simon's voicemail.

"Cam. You need to come home." He hadn't bothered to hide the irritation in his tone. "It looks like you're trying to evade the law by staying away. I'm not sure if you've seen the news, but the police are building a case against you. I'll be honest—I'm worried. I know you had nothing to do with John's crimes, but you need to come back. Where I can help you." He huffed into the phone. "This is serious. If Mulholland finds any more links to you and John's victims, he could put out a warrant for your arrest. Call me." After a moment of silence, he added, "Or better yet, come home!"

Cameron let out a deep breath and pushed open the door to the motel's front office. Valerie cracked a smile upon her return, probably hoping she had come back to talk more about wolves. Cameron moved toward the large map of Alaska on the wall beside her desk.

"Did you need something, dear?" Her tone was pleasant.

Cameron pointed to the location of Miles's family cabin on the map. "Are there any airports around here? I can't see any roads nearby when I searched online."

Valerie set down her novel and stepped toward the map. "No. No airports. The closest one would be in Eagle. That whole area is rugged terrain. Especially this time of year." She stopped beside Cameron and folded her arms. "Everything's buried in snow. It's a wilderness area. Even in summer, road access in those parts is very limited."

Summer. If Simon was right, she could be in jail before then. Cameron turned to her. "Could someone live out there?"

"No." She shook her head for emphasis, as if Cameron wasn't understanding. "It's too isolated. There's nothing out there other than wilderness in a severe climate. No power. No food supply. No civilization."

Cameron looked back at the map. "Could you get out there on a snowmobile?"

"I mean, we're talking dense forest, mountain peaks, valleys, rivers—although they're mostly frozen over. Wild animals. It would be tough, if not impossible. And you see how far that is from the closest town?" She pointed to a spot near the Canadian border. "That's about one hundred miles. To get through that much rough terrain, it would take more than a day. And there's more to worry about than subzero temperatures if you camped out there."

"Like what?"

She tapped her finger on the same spot Cameron had pointed out. "That's the area where the rabid wolf population has been sighted. Even Bear Grylls wouldn't go out there, sweetheart."

Cameron pressed her lips together. Her heart felt like it was sinking inside her chest. If she told the police where John was, John would make sure she went down with him for his crimes—and for her own. And if she waited until summer to go after him herself, she might already be unjustly jailed for being his accomplice. John would live out the rest of his days in off-grid freedom.

And if John was two hundred miles away, hiding out in the middle of the Yukon-Charly Rivers Preserve, then who had left the note in her motel room?

"What about the Yukon River?" Cameron pointed to the map. "Could you ride a snowmobile on it right now?"

Valerie nodded. "They travel on it for the Yukon Quest."

"What's that?"

Valerie raised her eyebrows. "You haven't heard of it? It's an international sled dog race. Held every February, and Eagle is one of their stops. It's about the only thing that brings in visitors this time of year, but the race won't get there for another couple of weeks." She elbowed Cameron gently. "Why are you asking about this area? You want to go wolf hunting now?"

"Something like that."

"Well, I'm glad I whetted your appetite." Valerie sauntered back to her chair behind the desk.

At the manager's mention of Bear Grylls, Cameron thought Valerie seemed like someone who could win one of those survival shows that were so popular. The ones John used to watch and brag about how he'd do it better if he were ever needy enough to go on one of them. Cameron had watched with him on occasion, but now she wished she'd paid better attention.

If she was going to make it, she was going to need to improve her winter survival skills. And fast.

"You know," Valerie said. "When I was a teenager, my friend's grandmother had a lake cabin, and her and I used to howl and get wild wolves to answer us."

Cameron turned away from the map.

"We could draw them to the shoreline when we were canoeing, or right up to the cabin door." Valerie pointed to the wall behind her. "Just beyond these woods. Howling is still what I do to draw out a wolf when I'm hunting them. And I tell you what: you howl when you're out on your trapline trip, and I guarantee you'll get a response from the wolves."

"I might just do that. Good night."

"Good night, dear," Valerie said as Cameron stepped out into the freezing night. "And enjoy that book!"

Cameron zipped her down coat up to her chin as she walked along the snowmobile tracks on the side of the road toward the Wolf Pack Bar. She'd only been outside for a few seconds and already felt accosted by the winter elements.

She had no winter survival skills. If she went up and tried to find John, chances were she would die. Which didn't seem that much worse than spending the rest of her life in jail—especially for something she didn't do. But that would leave John unpunished.

All she had was the element of surprise. At least she knew how to use a gun.

The warm air from inside the Wolf Pack Bar was a pleasant relief when she stepped inside. The place was busy, and the music was turned up. Cameron spotted Karl asleep in the booth Bethany's family had occupied that afternoon.

"Alaskan White?" Joan asked her when she reached the bar.

A couple of guys hollered from a nearby pool table.

Cameron draped her coat over the back of her barstool. "Let's make it a whiskey."

Joan slapped her hand atop the counter. "You got it."

"And I'll have a Coke."

Cameron turned toward the familiar voice, surprised to see Dane settle into the seat beside her.

CHAPTER TWENTY-NINE

"I thought you were in Fairbanks?"

Dane still wore his uniform, but he looked weary compared to when she'd seen him this morning. It struck her that she probably did, too.

He shook his head. "I never made it."

Joan set their drinks in front of them.

"Thanks," Cameron said.

Dane nodded to Joan, who disappeared across the bar before he continued in a lowered voice.

"The Fairbanks prison called not long after I spoke with you. The inmate who confessed to Bethany's murder hanged himself in his cell." He lifted his glass.

Cameron watched him take a drink from his Coke. "Did he give any details about Bethany's murder beforehand?"

"Not other than what was in the news."

"So, what does that mean?"

"He was in the area when Bethany went missing—spent the night at a truck stop in Dry Creek. It's about an hour away. His credit card wasn't used at the bar that night, but he could've been here and paid cash. Or grabbed Bethany in the parking lot after she closed down the bar."

"Do *you* think he did it?"

He took another large sip. "I'm not sure. Aside from him being in the vicinity the night Bethany disappeared, there's no other evidence to prove he was telling the truth. His cell phone records place him back in Fairbanks the next day, and he returned to work the day after that. I just came back from informing Bethany's parents. They took it hard. To find out we had a suspect and that he died before we could get answers." He stared into his glass. "We might never know for certain."

"Another Coke?" Joan asked, breaking his stare.

"No, thanks."

Joan glanced at Cameron's whiskey and stepped away. Her glass was still untouched. Cameron took a drink and tried not to make a face as the amber liquid burned the back of her mouth.

Dane swiveled his bar stool to face her. "How much longer are you staying in town?"

She cleared her throat. "Um. I'm not sure." She had no way to get to John. According to Simon, she needed to go home before Mulholland put out a warrant for her arrest. "Probably not much longer, right after the hunting trip," she added.

"I'm heading out for a couple days. I need to get away. Clear my head."

"Where are you going?"

"Ice fishing."

"What about the storm?"

"The snowfall ended up being much less than what was expected. We only got a few more inches. My dad's already complaining that I brought him back over nothing. Like he's forgotten if he hadn't gone to the dentist earlier, he could've died."

"You're going back to your cabin then?"

"No. There's a lake just south of here that's great for ice fishing. I'll drive and then snowmobile in the last bit."

"Oh." She forced down another swig of whiskey. "Do you have a cabin there, too?"

He smiled for the first time since he'd been at the bar. "I'll be camping."

Cameron choked on her drink.

His smile faded. "Are you all right?"

She set her glass on the counter. "*Camping?* In this weather?"

His grin returned. "Yeah. Winter camping. I have all the gear for it. It's fairly common around here."

"I didn't realize people did that. For fun."

"In this part of the world they do." He held out his hand and stood from his seat. "Well, if I don't see you before you leave, it was really nice to meet you, Shay. And thanks for flying me up to rescue my stubborn and unpleasant father."

She placed her hand in his, surprised by its warmth. "Oh, you're welcome. You know, your dad's got a certain charm to him."

Dane let out a big laugh. When he let go of her hand, Cameron felt that the moment had slipped away too quickly.

He moved for the door, and she watched him walk away. All at once, she realized what she needed to do.

She slid off her barstool and reached the trooper just before he left the bar. "Dane!" she called over the Neil Young song that played.

He turned.

"Can I go with you?"

He raised his eyebrows. "Ice fishing?"

"Yes. I've always wanted to go. And I still have a couple of days before my hunting trip."

"You want to camp in the snow?" A look of amusement came over his face. "You realize it's gonna be cold, right?"

Her parents had been avid backpackers, but the last time she'd camped with them was when she was in dental school. And she'd never camped in the winter.

"I know." She was aware of sounding overly eager, but she couldn't help it. This was the only way she'd have a chance at getting to John.

"I could probably drum up another sleeping bag for the tent. If you're sure you don't mind living outside in the Alaskan winter for a couple of days."

She smiled back at him. "Right now, there's nothing I'd rather do."

He placed his hand on the door. "Okay, then. We can leave tomorrow as soon as it's light. I'll pick you up at nine."

"Great."

"You want me to walk you back to your motel? You probably shouldn't be walking back alone."

After what happened to Bethany, he means.

Cameron waved her hand dismissively. "Thanks, but I'll be fine." *I lived with a serial killer,* she wanted to say. *If I lived through that….*

He lingered near the doorway for a moment, obviously uncomfortable with Cameron's decision.

"You don't need to worry about me," she added. "I'll be leaving soon. And I'll see you tomorrow."

"Okay," he finally said.

Cameron went back to the bar after Dane stepped outside. She finished her whiskey in two large gulps, wishing she'd asked for a water to chase it down.

"You want another?" Joan asked soon after she'd emptied her glass.

"No thanks. I'm heading out." She turned for the door.

"It's nice seeing you with Sergeant Waska," Joan said. "I haven't seen him with a woman since the accident."

Cameron looked back at Joan. She was about to ask what accident she was referring to when Joan moved across the bar.

"Hey boys!" Joan turned toward the two men playing pool. "Can one of you take Karl home when you're finished?"

"Sure," one of them said. "We're almost done."

Joan nodded before disappearing behind a doorway at the back of the bar. Cameron would have to ask her about the accident another time. Although, she supposed it really wasn't any of her business.

A bell chimed when she opened the door and stepped outside. Her breath was immediately visible under the lights that lit up the front of the bar. She walked through the mostly empty parking lot toward her motel, thinking of Bethany walking this same path the night she disappeared.

Cameron imagined John lurking in the dark, lying in wait for the beautiful young girl. She eyed the silhouette of a pickup in the middle of the parking lot and pictured John jumping out from behind Bethany's car, attacking her before she had a chance to climb inside.

Or maybe he charmed her. Stayed behind as the last patron and offered to help her take out the trash before he left. That seemed more like him.

She shivered, unsure if her body reacted to the cold or the thought of John. Her mind went back to the note left in her motel room. It wasn't John's handwriting, but she'd suspected he put someone up to it. But if he was hiding out in some off-grid cabin, there was no way he would know she was here.

She reached the edge of the parking lot and used the light from her phone to find the snowmobile tracks beside the road. There were no streetlamps. The only light came from the gas station across the street and the occasional passing car on the two-lane highway.

She was starting to see why Dane offered to take her back. Maybe living with a serial killer had made her feel invincible. She started down the tracks when an ice-cold hand clamped around her wrist from behind.

CHAPTER THIRTY

Cameron whipped around, pulling her arm away from her assailant's grip. A man stood behind her and raised up his gloveless hands in defense.

"Easy there," he drawled.

It was too dark to make out the man's face, but she recognized his drunken slur.

"Karl?"

"I didn't mean to frighten you." He dropped his hands to his sides. "But you shouldn't be walking alone at night out here. Didn't you hear what happened to Bethany?"

"Karl!" a voice called from the bar's parking lot.

A truck's engine rumbled and Cameron spotted a figure waving his arms in the glow of its taillights.

"Get back here, Karl!" the man shouted.

"You be careful now," Karl reminded her, before turning back for the truck.

Cameron watched him sway off the snowmobile tracks and walk through a pile of snow to get back to the parking lot where one of the men from the pool table was waiting for him.

"Sorry about that ma'am!" the man called out. "He's harmless."

"That's okay." Cameron waved and followed the path to the road.

The two blocks to her motel felt more like a mile in the frigid dark night. Cameron unlocked the door to her cabin and turned on the light. She leaned against the wall after closing the door behind her, relieved to be back inside her room. Stuffed wolf and all.

"I brought you some extra outer gear." Dane eyed Cameron's jeans and puffer coat from the driver's seat of his truck. "You won't be warm enough in those clothes."

"They might be a little big," he added. "But they'll keep you warm." He took a sip from his coffee thermos. "There's coffee in there for you." He motioned toward another thermos in the middle console.

"Thanks." Cameron reached for the insulated mug. Dane looked every bit the rugged outdoorsman in his insulated hunting jacket and wool hat. He was even more attractive out of his uniform, Cameron thought. Under different circumstances, it might have felt like they were on a date. Cameron looked out the window of Dane's truck as he turned off the Alaskan Highway.

After flipping through Valerie's book on wolves, she'd fallen asleep halfway through the night watching winter survival videos on YouTube, which only made her realize she was no match for this extreme wilderness in the winter. Hopefully her time with Dane would prove more useful.

"Where are we going again?"

Dane slowed as he drove through a large open gate and waved at a young woman who stepped out onto the porch of a tiny wood house the size of Cameron's garden shed in Laurelhurst.

"Tetlin Lake. We'll take this road to a little village up ahead by the same name. Then we'll take the snowmachine into the lake from there."

"What are you fishing for?"

"Lake trout, northern pike. If we get lucky maybe some whitefish."

Cameron spotted two animals on the side of the road with their heads down. Dane slowed to a stop when they got closer.

"Are those elk or moose?"

The animals lifted their heads toward the vehicle, exposing their broad sets of antlers. Cameron's jaw dropped in awe as the large creatures crossed the road in front of them. The tops of their antlers stood almost as high as the truck.

"Caribou." Dane stepped on the gas once the road was clear. "Moose are actually much bigger. You definitely don't want to hit one of those."

Cameron turned her head to watch the caribou as they drove away.

"Tetlin is inside a national wildlife refuge. There's all kinds of animals out here: Canadian lynx, bears, turkey vultures, red fox, wolf packs...."

She faced forward in her seat. "That sounds kind of dangerous."

He smiled. "We'll be careful. I brought a gun. The bears are hibernating, and it's very rare for wolves to attack humans."

"Unless they have rabies."

Dane shot her a sideways glance. "How'd you know that?"

"My motel manager is obsessed with wolves."

"Oh, right." He let out a short laugh. "Valerie's a hell of a hunter."

"*Mmm.* And decorates with them." She couldn't help but laugh herself. "But really, what is it with this place and wolves? I mean, there's the Wolf Pack Bar, the Howling Wolf Motel. There's even a stuffed wolf in my motel room."

They reached the Village of Tetlin, settled around a frozen winding river. It consisted mostly of homes scattered amidst the forestland with a few larger structures in the middle of the village.

"My dad was born in this village," Dane said. "And unlike the fairy tales you probably heard growing up, where wolves are villains, the natives here teach their children to revere wolves for their strength—and vicious hunting skills." Dane turned onto a narrow road at the edge of the town. "My ancestors believed wolves should be honored for their bravery and tried to imitate wolves' hunting patterns. But you're right, Valerie—your motel manager—is obsessed."

The road ended and Dane parked at a small trailhead. They got out of the truck, and Cameron looked on as he started the snowmobile. The engine rumbled to life, and he backed it off the trailer. He pulled a sled from his truck bed— piled high with gear—and connected it to the back of the snowmobile.

Cameron tried to imagine doing this herself.

"That's a lot of gear," she said.

He tightened a strap over the top of a large bin containing supplies. "I usually take a bit less and keep it pretty primitive, but since you were coming, I thought I'd make things a little more comfortable. Here." He handed her a navy snowsuit and a pair of winter gloves. "That should fit over your clothes."

She sat on the end of the truck bed and stepped into the snowsuit. She pulled the heavy-duty gloves over her leather ones. Fortunately, her Sorel boots were one thing she owned that was actually made for this weather. Dane grabbed a coat from the cab and pulled it on over his hunting jacket.

"Ready?" He grabbed two helmets from the back of the snowmobile and held one out to her.

She accepted the helmet and pulled it on, lowering the shield over her face after adjusting the strap. "Would you mind if I drive?"

"You ever ridden one of these before?"

"Nope."

"Okay, sure." He flipped up the visor on his helmet and pointed to a lever on the right side of the handlebars. "This is the throttle." Then he pointed to the left handlebar. "And that's your brake. You steer it the same way you would a bike, and you might have to lean into the corners if it doesn't turn enough. Sound good?"

She gave him a gloved thumbs up. Dane turned and jumped on the snowmobile then slid to the back of the seat. She climbed on in front of him.

She could feel the warmth of his body behind her as she gently squeezed the throttle and started down the narrow trail through the woods.

"You can go a little faster if you want!" Dane yelled over the engine, as they crept along the snowmobile trail.

Cameron gradually pressed harder on the throttle until the trees passed in a blur on either side of them.

"There you go!" Dane called from behind her.

She leaned into the corners, increasing their speed as she navigated through the winding trail. Her thoughts drifted to John, thinking of him enjoying this winter landscape while he left her to pay for his crimes. She tightened her grip on the throttle, and they sped toward the next bend in the trail.

"Whoa! Slow down for that turn!"

She pressed her thumb hard on the throttle, not registering Dane's words.

CHAPTER THIRTY-ONE

"Shay! Slow down!"

Dane's gloved hand reached past hers and pressed the brake lever. The snowmobile slowed as they started through the turn. But even with the brake, they were going too fast to make the tight corner. Cameron leaned to the right and let up on the throttle as the snowmobile veered off the trail and skidded up onto a mound of snow. The sled they towed behind them smacked against a tree as they came to a stop.

Cameron was breathing hard, but not from nearly plowing into the trees. Her anger for John surged within her.

"So, maybe not quite that fast." Dane's voice was calm over the idling engine. "You want me to drive now?"

"No, I'm good."

She pressed the gas again and they flew down the snow mound back onto the trail.

"Just take it a little easier this time!" he shouted.

The trees cleared and gave way to the lake, which was about the same size as the one she'd landed on two days ago. She stopped when they neared the edge of the frozen water.

"Keep going!" Dane said.

"Onto the lake?" Cameron's body tensed.

Dane laughed. "We can't ice fish from shore."

How thick was the ice?

"Are you sure it can hold us?"

"Yes. Don't worry. You could drive a truck on this lake. It's just like at my cabin. Watch."

His right hand gripped around hers on the throttle. Before she could react, the snowmobile sped onto the ice.

She screamed as they soared atop the frozen surface. "Dane!"

When they reached the middle of the lake, he released her hand from his. He reached in front of her and killed the engine.

"See? Plenty thick."

He offered his hand to help her off, but she folded her arms. "We could've died."

He laughed. "No, we couldn't have. And to be fair, you gave me quite a scare back there, too."

Cameron couldn't help but grin as she climbed off the snowmobile. "Thanks for letting me drive." She looked back toward the trail. "Can't we fish a little closer to shore? I don't like being all the way out here with all that weight." She pointed to the snowmobile and overloaded trailer.

Dane pulled off his helmet and grinned. "It's fine. You'll see how thick the ice is when I drill the holes."

He lifted a snow shovel from the trailer and started to clear snow from the ice. Cameron didn't understand why he hadn't just parked the snowmobile on the shore. It seemed risky to leave it on the ice, even it was thick.

"Are you sure this is safe?" she asked, after Dane had cleared a square patch of snow from the ice.

"Don't worry, I've been fishing this lake my whole life. And I've never fallen through the ice. The outside temperature won't get above ten degrees for another month or so." He pulled a corkscrew the size of a weedwhacker out of the sled. "Watch."

"I thought that was for the wine."

Dane winked at her and hefted the auger to his shoulder, taking a few steps toward Cameron. He set the auger on the ice, and with a few pulls on the cord, the motor fired up. Cameron took a few steps back, afraid to be too close, and covered her ears. She watched the spinning blades cut through the frozen surface, creating a pile of shaved ice around it. Dane bent over as the blade continued to sink beneath the surface. Nearly the entire blade had disappeared into the ice when water suddenly sloshed out of the hole. Cameron jumped back, thinking for sure they were going under.

Dane stood up straight as he withdrew the auger from the water. "See? Come look."

Cameron took slow steps toward him and peered into the hole from a few feet away, even though Dane's feet were only inches from the edge.

"The ice this time of year is more than two feet thick, closer to three. It's perfectly safe."

"Okay…if you say so."

Now that he had convinced her they were not going to drown any minute, Dane drilled another hole just a few feet away from the first, then cut the motor.

She watched him pull a long canvas bag from the storage bin. He dropped it onto the ice where he'd cleared the snow, and Cameron realized it housed a tent. Dane knelt beside it and lifted his head in her direction.

"I'm going to set up the shack first, to keep us warm, then we'll get some lines in the water."

"We're sleeping out *here*?"

"Well, yeah. We can fish all night if you want."

Cameron searched his face for a sign he was joking. "On the *ice*?" There was no way she was going to spend the night on a frozen lake.

With one fluid motion, Dane reached inside the shack and pulled it over his head, popping the support poles in place.

He wasn't joking. They were going to sleep atop the frozen lake. She swallowed and stepped toward him.

"How do you know we won't fall through?"

Dane unzipped the door to the shack and popped his head out. "I do this all the time."

Once the ice shack was standing, Dane went to the supply sled and withdrew a black object from the bin.

"Wait. What's that?" Cameron asked, as he carried it inside the tent. Even though she knew exactly what it was. She just couldn't understand how they could have a fire without melting the ice beneath them.

"A woodstove," he said. "It's how we'll keep warm. I normally just use the propane heater, but I didn't want you to be cold."

Cameron followed him into the shack. She watched him set the stove on the ice and poke the chimney out a hole cut into the top.

"Won't that melt the ice underneath us?"

He shook his head. "Heat rises. So, the warm air will go up." He lifted his hands in the air.

"Have you done this before? With the stove?"

He smiled. "Yeah, since I was a little kid. We'll get some brush to lay between the base of the stove and the ice. It will keep the heat from melting it." He put his hand on her shoulder, seeing the worried look on her face. "Trust me. We'll be fine."

Cameron bit her lip and stared at the stove.

"Do you mind gathering up some branches from the shore and bringing them back here while I finish setting everything up? There's a small handsaw in the sled."

Her eyes met Dane's after she tore them away from the stove.

"Sure," she said, still wondering how Dane could be so confident. She'd been hoping to watch him build a fire in the snowy woods. If she *did* go after John, there was no way she could take a stove with her.

A male voice crackled from Dane's waist, making Cameron jump.

"462 Dispatch: respond to Alaska Highway and Dogsled Drive for a single vehicle collision reporting minor injuries."

Dane pulled a handheld radio from his pocket and turned down the volume. "Didn't mean to startle you."

"Are you on call or something?"

He slid the radio back into his pocket as a female voice came over the frequency. "No, I just like to be aware of what's going on in town. And there's no cell service out here, so it's good to have in case of emergency."

Cameron swallowed. "Like falling through the ice?"

Dane chuckled as he followed her out of the tent. "We won't fall through the ice. I promise. A lot of times I come out here alone, so it's good to have a way to communicate. In fact, if we continued out much farther, even my radio wouldn't work. A lot of the areas where we respond to calls is outside of our radio range."

"Really? What if you needed backup or something?"

"All the troopers out here carry a satellite phone for when we get out of range. You can't call, but you can text. And it takes about five minutes to send."

"That seems dangerous."

"It's just the way it is up here."

She found the handsaw in the sled near the top of the supplies.

"Don't go too far," he called as she headed for the shore. "You should be able to find what we need right along here."

Cameron gave him a thumbs up and headed for the trees that lined the lake, glad for an excuse to get off the frozen surface. She wandered along the shore and pulled a fallen branch out from under the snow. She shook it off. *Was this what Dane meant by brush?*

There's no way I can get to John by myself. I don't have a clue what I'm doing. She was a *dentist*, not a survivalist. If she died in the wilderness trying to get to him, John would win. She was probably better off going back to face Mulholland.

She looked back at Dane. He unfolded a cot and slid it inside the tent. Maybe she should tell him the truth, and he could help her get to John. But when John told the police what she'd done to her first husband, who would want to protect her then?

She stepped into the forest where the snowfall had been sheltered by the trees and branches protruded through the snow. She grabbed a small one, shook it off, and moved deeper into the woods. She stopped and sawed the base of a low hanging branch. It fell partway off. She gripped it with both hands and leaned her body weight backward.

The branch gave way with a loud snap. Behind her, Cameron heard a huff followed by a throaty, grunting sound. She turned. The branches fell from her hands.

An animal bigger than she'd ever seen glared at her from less than ten feet away. With its eyes fixed on Cameron, the moose bowed its head, exposing its pointed antlers. Cameron stood still, afraid if she moved she would antagonize the huge beast even more.

The moose huffed air out its nostrils again and reared onto its hind legs.

"Dane!"

The moose kicked its long front legs, punching the air with its hooves, and charged toward her.

CHAPTER THIRTY-TWO

"I'm Detective Sergeant Cox."

Tanner accepted the man's handshake in the lobby of the Sequim Police Department. "Thanks for meeting with me."

"No problem, Detective. Come on back."

Tanner followed the man through the newly constructed building to a spacious office in the back. Cox closed the door and handed Tanner a manila folder before taking a seat in an ergonomic chair behind his wooden desk. The snow-capped Olympic mountains were visible in the distance beyond the large window behind him. Tanner opened the folder and sat down across from him.

"So, Miles Henson's widow went on to marry the Teacher Killer? Wow, she's got some great taste in men."

Tanner flipped through the pages inside the folder and looked up at Cox. "Is this all there is?"

The detective sergeant's grin faded. "Yeah. Like I said on the phone, it was a cut-and-dried case. Not sure it was worth your time driving over here. I could've sent this all by email."

Tanner closed the file. "I wanted to speak with you in person, since you were the lead investigator in Miles Henson's death."

"Everything you need to know is in there. The coroner ruled his death a suicide. The guy poured gasoline all over the house and lit it on fire before he shot himself."

Tanner watched Cox swivel side to side in his chair. He couldn't be much more than thirty-five, which would've made him a rookie detective when Miles died. Possibly even his first investigation.

"I noticed in the autopsy report that there was no evidence of smoke inhalation in Henson's lungs."

The young detective sergeant shrugged his shoulders. "He could've set fire to the place right before he pulled the trigger. The bullet killed him instantly."

"He was a dentist," Cox continued. "His employees had noticed him drinking on the job. His wife said he was depressed and drank heavily at home. His body was too severely burned to obtain a blood alcohol level, but there were two liquor bottles found near his body. Case closed."

"Did you interview any of Cameron Henson's employees or friends to find out what their relationship was like?"

"No." Cox's answer was immediate. "Didn't see any need."

"Do you recall if Miles and Cameron Henson worked at the same dental practice?"

"They were separate. Miles had his own dental practice and Cameron worked at a joint practice with another dentist."

226

"Is her practice still around?"

"Yes, the office is still open—I'm a patient there actually. It's only a few blocks up the road. But the dentist Cameron was partnered with at the time died a few years back of a heart attack. I'm not sure if there's anyone still working at the office who was around when she was there."

"Thanks for your time." Tanner stood.

Cox followed him to the door. "Sorry I can't give you anything else. I know you're looking into a criminal history for Cameron Prescott, but—trust me—Miles Henson killed himself. The investigation was thorough."

Tanner opened the door, a new plan already in mind.

"It may not be my place," Cox added, "but I think you're grasping at straws here on this one."

Tanner reviewed the case file in his Ford Fusion before going to the dental office. Tucked inside the rain shadow of the Olympic Mountains, the seaside town had awarded itself the nickname *Sunny Sequim*. The midday sun reflected brightly against his windshield, despite it being February in Washington.

Tanner stopped on the crime scene photos of Miles Henson's charred body and chewed his gum with increasing speed. He held up the photo and wondered why this hadn't been mentioned in the coroner's autopsy report. Miles had been found slumped over—sideways on his couch—with his pistol still in his grip.

Tanner studied the angle of Henson's arm. If Henson's bullet wound was instantly fatal, the odds that the gun would've remained in his grip after he died were minute, if not impossible. Tanner closed the file and placed it on the floor of his passenger seat before getting out of his car. He'd get a second consult with the Seattle medical examiner when he got back.

He walked the three blocks to Cameron's old dental practice, enjoying the sun on his face. Two people looked up from their seats in the waiting room as he moved to the front desk.

"Do you have an appointment?" the middle-aged receptionist asked.

"No. I'm Detective Tanner Mulholland from Seattle Homicide, and I'm wondering if there's anyone still working here who worked for Doctor Cameron Prescott—I mean, formerly known as Cameron Henson—when she had this practice?"

The woman straightened when he said the word *homicide*. Then again when he said Cameron's name. It made him think that Cox was right. There wasn't anyone still working here who knew Cameron back then.

"Oh. Um, yes. I wasn't here then, but one of our hygienists was. She's been so upset to see Cameron's name in the news. Would you like to speak with her?"

He flashed her a pleasant smile. "I would."

The receptionist brought him back to wait in the dentist's empty office. A few minutes later, a blonde woman in scrubs appeared in the doorway.

"I'm Tina," she said. "You wanted to speak with me about Cameron?"

Tanner held out his hand. "I'm Detective Mulholland from Seattle Homicide. Yes, thank you."

"Sure." She accepted his handshake.

There was only one chair in the room, but neither of them sat.

"So, you worked for Cameron when her first husband died?"

She nodded.

"Did you know her very well?"

"A little. We went out a few times after work, but Miles didn't like it. He would call her the whole time until she'd finally say she had to go home. Once, after we went out for a drink, I saw bruises on her arm the next morning. I asked what happened, and she said she ran into something. But her bruises looked like fingerprints. I asked if everything was okay at home, but she insisted things were fine. I stopped inviting her to go out after that. I didn't want to cause problems for her."

"Did you tell the police any of this after Miles died?"

She shook her head. "They never spoke to me. And after he killed himself, I figured there wasn't much point."

"How was Cameron after Miles died?"

She crossed her arms. "What do you mean?"

"Losing a spouse like that could be pretty devastating."

"Devastating?" Tina glanced out the open doorway before closing the office door. "Not if he was beating the crap out of you. Cameron was relieved, I could tell. And if

229

the guy was pushing her around like that, I don't blame her. I know it's a horrible thing to say, but I've always seen Miles's death as him doing her a favor." She chewed her lip. "Until I saw that she went on to marry The Teacher Killer. It's so awful."

Tanner thanked Tina for her time. He withdrew his sunglasses from his pocket when he stepped outside, thinking about what the hygienist had said about Miles doing Cameron a favor. He popped a fresh stick of gum in his mouth as he walked toward his car.

It seemed more likely that Cameron had done herself a favor.

CHAPTER THIRTY-THREE

A guttural sound erupted from the moose as it bolted toward Cameron. There was no time to run. Cameron crouched down and instinctively covered her head with her hands. Branches cracked under the animal's hooves as it stampeded straight at her. Her body tensed as she braced for being trampled upon. *This is how I'm going to die?*

A gunshot blasted through the forest from the edge of the tree line. Cameron lifted her hands in time to see the moose's head jerk backward. The animal landed in a heap beside her, the tips of its antlers only an inch from her face. The brush underneath her shook from the weight of the moose's fall.

"Shay!" Dane ran through the woods and knelt beside her, holding the stock of his rifle in his grip. "Are you hurt?"

She pushed herself up from the blood-covered snow with trembling hands. "I'm fine."

Dane put his arm around her and helped her to her feet. Cameron stared down at the massive animal. Each antler stretched longer than Cameron's legs. A puddle of blood pooled beneath its head. Dane had shot it straight through the temple.

This guy's a good shot. She turned away from the moose. "How did you get over here so fast?" There had only been seconds between the time she screamed his name and when he shot the moose.

Dane looked nearly as shaken as her. Maybe even more so. She was surprised to see the color had drained from his face, and he looked like he'd seen a ghost. "I lost sight of you, and I realized I shouldn't have sent you off by yourself without a gun. I was already headed this way when I heard you yell. I'm sorry—this was my fault."

"Don't be sorry. You saved me." Cameron looked at the huge animal lying at their feet. "What will we do with the moose?"

He pulled out his radio. "I'll have to notify the wildlife trooper in Tok. It's not hunting season, so I can't keep it. But they'll salvage the meat and donate it to someone on Alaska's roadkill waiting list."

Cameron wrinkled her nose. "There's a *roadkill* waiting list? That sounds appetizing."

"Moose are really good eating. Trust me. Even a city girl like you would like it."

"I think I'll stick with chicken."

He grinned. Cameron stared at the moose while Dane made the radio call. It was bigger than a horse.

A male voice came over the radio. "Copy that. Sounds like a close call. Can you bring the animal back to town or do you need us to come to you?"

"I'm going to need you to come and get it. I'd have to quarter it to get it onto my sled, and I don't have the gear to do that."

Cameron's eyes widened, thinking of Dane slicing the animal into pieces.

"What's your location?"

"You'll see my truck parked at the trailhead to Tetlin Lake and you can follow my snowmachine tracks to the lake." Dane pulled a small black device from one of his pockets. "I brought my GPS," he said and read off their coordinates. "But you'll see us when you get to the lake."

"Just give me about an hour."

Dane turned to Cameron after signing off. "Come on. Let's head back to our camp."

Cameron followed him out of the woods, relieved to get away from the animal that almost killed her. They moved across the lake, and Cameron saw smoke blowing out the stove pipe that stuck out the side of their tent.

"Here." Dane removed the shoulder strap of his gun and held out his rifle toward her. "You should probably know how to use this while we're out here."

"Oh. I don't..." Cameron looked down at the firearm. She knew how to use it. John had taught her how to shoot his hunting rifle at their cabin. Before that, she'd learned how to shoot a pistol out of necessity. But she couldn't think of how to explain that without telling Dane too much.

"Please, just take it. I'll show you how to shoot. And you'll need to take your glove off so you can pull the trigger."

Dane held up one of his hands. The tips of his gloves were folded back to expose his fingers. "Mine are made for hunting."

After pulling the glove off her right hand, she slipped it into her coat pocket. Reluctantly, she took the rifle into her hands, gripping the barrel with her gloved hand and the stock with her other.

Dane moved around behind her. "Okay, so press the butt of the gun against your right shoulder and grip the handle with your right hand, but don't put your finger on the trigger yet."

Cameron followed his directions, aiming the gun at the woods from where they'd just come.

"Then use your left hand to hold the stock beneath the barrel."

She could feel the warmth of Dane's breath on the side of her face. "Like this?" She intentionally moved her hand too far back.

"Hold it out farther." Dane gently guided her hand toward the front of the stock. "There. That's perfect." He pointed to a silver knob above the trigger. "This is the bolt handle. Use your right hand to lift it up and pull it toward you."

She slid it back, exposing a cartridge inside the barrel.

"Now slide it forward."

After chambering the round, Cameron rotated the bolt handle down.

Dane stepped back. "Okay, see that big tree over there?" He pointed to the edge of the lake. "That biggest one right next to where we came through with the snowmachine."

"I see it."

"Look through the scope and line up the crosshairs until it's aimed at the middle of that tree."

Cameron closed one eye and centered the crosshairs on the tree trunk.

"Now, before you put your finger on the trigger, you have to click the safety off. That's the little silver knob there.

"Ok, I got it."

"Great. Now get your aim back and gently pull the trigger when you're ready."

Cameron slid her finger onto the trigger and fired. The gun kicked. Her ears rang from the blast that echoed through the quiet wilderness.

Dane squinted toward the tree and turned to her. "Wow. You have good aim. You hit it right in the center." He stepped toward. "I'm impressed, city girl. You're a natural."

He grinned at her when she handed him the gun. She shrugged her shoulders. "Beginner's luck."

He ejected the casing and chambered another round. She watched him flip the safety before he slung the rifle back over his shoulder.

"You ready to catch some fish?"

A light snow began to fall as she trekked beside Dane toward the middle of the lake. A sharp crack sounded beneath the ice. Cameron stopped.

"What was that?" She looked down at her feet.

"Oh, it's nothing." Dane kept walking. "The ice must've shifted a bit. That's normal. It expands and contracts all the time due to the weather."

Cameron reluctantly followed him the rest of the way to the shack.

Before going inside, Dane retrieved a pair of binoculars from the sled and scanned the tree line along the shore.

"What are you looking for?" Cameron asked. It was too soon for the wildlife trooper to be there.

He lowered the binoculars. "Just making sure no animals start feeding off that moose before Trooper Nelson comes."

Cameron turned and examined the trees that lined the frozen lake, thinking of the gigantic moose lying dead in the forest and all the dangers that lurked inside these woods. *What am I still doing here?* If it weren't for Dane, she would have died.

She should go back to Seattle and tell Simon what she'd done to her first husband. And let him defend her against the criminal charges that Mulholland would likely bring against her.

"If the clouds clear, we'll have a great view of the Northern Lights tonight."

Dane stepped inside the shack, and she followed behind him. A fire burned in the woodstove, and it was already comfortably warm. Cameron warily eyed the slush beneath the stove.

"I didn't bring back any brush," she said.

"It's okay, we can get it later. It's not going to melt through. It just might get a little wet."

Cameron backed away from the fire and sat beside Dane on the cot.

He held a short fishing pole in one hand and dropped the baited line into the dark hole. "You want to fish?" He held the pole toward her.

"Sure." As she accepted the pole, she couldn't help but think that the last time she went fishing was with John on their honeymoon in Mexico.

"You have a boyfriend waiting for you back in Portland?"

Cameron turned to him. His dark eyes waited for her answer.

"No." She shook her head. "It's just me."

"When you feel that hit the bottom, reel up a little."

Cameron felt a bite as soon as she started to reel. She jerked the tip up and reeled, feeling the fight from the end of the line.

"You got one already?" Dane laughed. "Damn!"

She kept reeling against the weight of the fish. "It feels big."

"When it gets closer, you'll have to work its head up through the hole. But watch so the line doesn't get caught up on the ice. That can break the line."

She felt a rush of excitement as the fish came up through the deep column of ice. She lifted the pole to the top of the shack when she spotted the sinker come out of the water. There was a splash before a tiny silver fish broke the surface.

"Looks like a little trout," Dane said, as it flopped on the ice.

"I thought it was going to be bigger." Cameron stared at her catch. It was no more than six inches long.

"These little guys can be feisty." Dane lifted the fish with one hand, slid the hook out of its mouth, and held it toward Cameron. "Nice catch."

Cameron leaned back and Dane gently released it into the hole. They watched it disappear into the dark water. He rebaited the little jig with another worm before dropping the line back down the hole.

She remembered what Joan had said about Dane not being the same since *the accident*.

"How about you?"

"Yeah, I better get fishing or you're going to outdo me your first time out."

"No…I mean, do you live alone?"

"Yeah." He stared at the hole in the ice. "I was married once. A long time ago."

"What happened?"

"She was killed in a car accident. Hit by a truck when she pulled out onto the Alaskan Highway in front of the trooper station…I was the first one on scene."

"I'm so sorry." Cameron rested her gloved hand on his arm, struck by the sadness in his voice. How awful it must be for him to have to see the place she was killed every day.

Was that why he looked so shaken after he killed the moose?

When he turned toward her, their faces were only inches apart. "She would've liked you."

Conflicting emotions surged inside her. She wanted to tell him that she knew what it was like to lose someone you loved, but realized it wasn't true. John hadn't died and she didn't love him, she'd only thought she had.

Dane leaned toward her. Why couldn't she have met him instead of John all those years ago? Their lips were almost touching. She shouldn't allow herself to feel this way. She needed to stay focused on getting to John. On stopping him. But she couldn't bring herself to pull away.

She put her mouth to his. Their lips parted, and his tongue found hers. He leaned closer to her, and it took the last of her willpower to pull away.

"Dane," she breathed. "There's something I need to tell—"

"462 Dispatch. Respond to 68 Bear Creek Road for a possible overdose. Victim is a sixteen-year-old female found unresponsive."

Dane sat up and grabbed his radio from his pocket. He turned up the volume as the dispatcher continued.

"We are also sending EMS."

He stood up and stared wide-eyed at Cameron. "That's Bethany's parents' address."

Cameron's heart felt heavy with shock and disbelief. *Grace.*

Dane tucked the radio back into his pocket and reeled in his fishing line. "I need to go back."

"Of course."

Cameron brought her hand to her mouth. Their kiss was now all but forgotten. As Dane put out the fire, Cameron folded up the cots and placed them in the back of the sled.

CHAPTER THIRTY-FOUR

"Are you sure you don't want me to drop you off at your motel?"

"Yes. I can walk."

They'd met the wildlife trooper at the trailhead parking lot, and Dane told him to call him if they had any trouble finding the moose. On their drive back from the lake, they had heard over Dane's police scanner that Grace had been transported to the town's medical center by the emergency responders, who were attempting to revive her.

Dane turned onto the Tok Cutoff, and Cameron spotted the ambulance parked in front of the medical center up the road. Clouds loomed in the wide-open sky above. The facility looked newly constructed and was the largest building Cameron had seen in the town so far.

She reached for Dane's hand. His fingers enclosed around hers. Neither of them had spoken much on their trip back to town. Her thoughts were consumed with worry for Bethany's sister and parents, as well as a growing hatred for John.

He pulled into the clinic parking lot as Grace's parents emerged out a side door of the facility. Cameron watched Grace's father pull his wife into his arms as her body heaved with intense sobs.

Please let Grace be alive.

Cameron sucked in a sharp breath when a stretcher was wheeled out of the clinic with a closed black body bag lying on top. Grace's father turned away and buried his face into the side of his wife's head. Cameron brought her hand to her mouth.

"Oh, shit."

Cameron turned to Dane's grief-stricken face. He closed his eyes and clenched his jaw. She knew what he must be thinking. That the catalyst of Grace's suicide was the news of the inmate's confession that was snuffed away by his death, which meant they might never know the truth about Bethany.

"I'm so sorry, Dane."

She looked back to the medics loading Grace's body into the back of an ambulance. But Cameron knew the truth about who killed Bethany. She knew it without a doubt.

"I'll call you as soon as I can." Dane leaned forward and kissed her softly before opening his side door. He left the engine running. "Why don't you take my truck back to your motel? I'll come get it later."

Cameron nodded. It ripped at her heart to know this would be the last time she ever saw him. How could this be so painful when she only met him a few days ago? If only things were different.

She climbed into the driver's seat, thinking how she almost told him who she was up at the lake. She was glad now she hadn't. Because no one could know what she was about to do.

"I'll see you soon," Dane called before jogging toward the parked ambulance.

But as Grace's parents solemnly climbed into the ambulance with their daughter's body, she knew what had to be done. Cameron watched Dane climb in behind them. She waited until the ambulance turned onto the Alaskan Highway before she pulled Dane's truck out of the parking lot.

Cameron parked Dane's truck beside her Cessna at the Tok Junction Airport. She grabbed the gallon of water off the front seat she'd bought at the town's grocery store, along with a paper bag filled with sports drinks and protein bars. After loading the food supplies into the back of her plane, she gathered all the winter camping supplies from the back of Dane's truck that she could fit into her plane's storage compartment.

The wood stove was too big to take, but she found a small propane heater and threw it in among her supplies, along with a few bottles of fuel. Lastly, she grabbed his rifle and a small box of ammo. She set the gun and bullets in the backseat of her plane, then remembered seeing a pair of handcuffs in Dane's glove compartment. She went back to the truck and left Dane's key fob on the passenger seat after taking the handcuffs.

When she had stopped at the motel to pick up her belongings, she'd used the phone in her room to call the only motel in Eagle and arranged for them to pick her up from the airport when she landed. While on the phone, Cameron had spotted Valerie's wolf book on the nightstand. She tucked it inside her bag as a plan began to form in her mind. Finally, she turned her cellphone off in case Dane tried to track her number when he found out she'd left with all his camping gear.

Cameron tore her eyes from the truck. *It has to be this way,* she told herself. And if Dane knew John like she did, and what he'd done, he'd understand. She wondered if he was still with Grace's parents. Her heart broke remembering their faces as they watched Grace's body get loaded into the ambulance. She tried to force them from her mind as she focused on the surrounding skies above the snowy wilderness and how she was going to get to John. And keep him from hurting anyone ever again.

The sun was setting behind the mountainous horizon when she landed on the small airstrip beside the winding, snow-covered Yukon River. She'd thought about flying over Miles's family cabin, but she didn't want to risk John spotting her plane. From the air, Eagle made Tok look like a metropolis.

She'd flown over nothing but rugged forestland for the entire flight. When she got close to Eagle, she could see snowmobile tracks in the surrounding wilderness. It scared her to think she'd be going out there alone in the morning.

She grabbed her duffel bag after tying up the plane, leaving the camping gear and groceries inside. The motel van was the only vehicle parked beside the runway, making it easy to spot. An older man wearing a parka and knit cap greeted her when she got closer.

"I'm Roger. We spoke on the phone," he said. "I can take your bag."

"Thank you." Cameron slung the bag off her shoulder.

"Please, feel free to sit up front."

Cameron climbed inside the warm van while the driver put her bag in the back.

"You're a bit early for the Yukon Quest," Roger said, when he got in beside her.

He pulled onto a two-lane road. It was flanked by small evergreens, reminding Cameron of the roads in Tok.

"I'm just here for a night. Is there somewhere I could rent a snowmobile?"

"Not for a couple of weeks. The only rental place in town is closed until the Yukon Quest comes through. It's about the only thing that brings in visitors this time of year."

There had to be somewhere she could get one. "Do you know anyone in town who would rent me theirs for a few days? I could pay."

The driver wrinkled his brows. "I thought you were just here for the night?"

Cameron was beginning to miss the city where everyone was too busy to do anything but mind their own business. "I'm staying with a friend. Up the river."

"In Circle? That's a long way away."

The trees cleared when they entered the small town. "So, do you know where I might be able to find someone willing to rent me theirs?"

"I don't know. I mean, I have one. But it's fairly new, so I wouldn't feel real comfortable lending it out."

Cameron added up how much cash she still had with her. "How about for one thousand a day?"

Roger slowed for a four-way stop before turning into the motel parking lot. Cameron recognized the two-story building on the riverbank from the photo online.

"I don't know…."

"I can leave you the keys to my plane. As a deposit. Until I get back."

"Okay. Fine. But I want the cash up front."

"You got it. Thank you."

Cameron was relieved when he got out of the van without asking any more questions.

"Follow me," he said, after he retrieved her duffel bag from the back.

The motel lobby was empty when they went inside. She followed the man to the front desk where he stepped behind the counter and checked her into her room. She looked around. *Was he the only one working here?*

"So, just the one night?" he asked.

Cameron turned. "That's right."

"I'll need to put a credit card on file or a hundred-dollar cash deposit."

After she handed him the cash, he pointed to a room at the front of the hotel.

"There's a café in there that serves dinner until seven. And we have a small convenience store at the other end of the motel."

"Thanks." Cameron slung her bag over her shoulder.

"What time do you want the snowmachine?"

"As soon as it gets light."

"I'll have it here by nine."

She anticipated it taking her almost two days to get to John. She pulled out nearly all the cash she had left from her Pacific Bank envelope and set it on the counter. "I'll need it for three days."

He nodded after counting the cash. "It's a deal. And the plane keys?"

"I'll leave them with you in the morning." Cameron turned for the convenience store, surprised to hear the man follow behind her.

"If you need the convenience store, I'll have to unlock it for you," he said. "Other than the café, I'm the only one working the hotel right now."

Cameron stepped inside the store after Roger opened the door for her. He moved behind the sales counter while Cameron looked around. It was a mix of groceries, souvenirs, and hunting and fishing gear.

Cameron turned to Roger. "Do you have any topographical maps of the area?"

"Sure do." He leaned over and withdrew a folded paper from behind the counter.

Bags of moose jerky were displayed on one of the aisle ends. Cameron slid one of the bags off the shelf, thinking of Dane, and the huge animal he'd killed to save her. She kept the bag and noticed a sign below it for wolf call howlers. They were black and the size of a small telescope. She picked one up and moved toward Roger when she spotted bear traps hanging from the wall. She stopped to look at the metal contraptions.

She turned to him. "Are these real? Or just souvenirs?"

He moved around the desk. "They're all real. I weld them myself—it's my hobby. Although, most people buy them to take home and mount on their walls."

"Do they work?"

"Well, yeah." Roger let out a chuckle. "But don't go home and use it on your husband or anything."

Cameron smiled. "He'll love it. Do you also by chance have a compass?"

CHAPTER THIRTY-FIVE

Tanner pulled into the Sequim gas station that Cameron had used as her alibi during Miles's time of death. He went inside and pulled a Gatorade from the refrigerator.

He wandered the aisle and slowed as he eyed the plastic gas cans, before going to the register. The arson investigation of the fire at Miles and Cameron's home revealed the presence of gasoline in the living room surrounding Miles's body, and a charred gas can was found near his remains.

When he got to the counter, a teenage girl took out one of her wireless earbuds while bobbing her head to the music apparently coming from the one in her other ear.

"Just this?" She lifted his Gatorade.

"Actually, I was wondering if there is anyone still working here who worked here about ten or eleven years ago?" He knew it was way too far back to get any surveillance footage from that night. But you never knew, he might get lucky and someone would remember her.

The girl behind the counter shook her head as she rang up his Gatorade. "Sorry. This place got a new owner about five years ago. And all the staff have been here less than that. Wait...." She pulled out her other earbud. "A woman already called a few days ago asking for our security footage from back then. I told her it only goes back ninety days."

"A woman? Did she give her name?"

"No. Why? Did something happen here? Like some sort of crime?"

"Not here, no." Tanner pulled his business card out of his wallet after paying for his Gatorade. "Could you give this to your store owner and ask them to call me? I just have a few questions."

Her eyes widened when she looked up after reading his card. "Sure."

"Thanks." Mulholland put on his sunglasses when he stepped outside. He'd get a warrant for the convenience store's phone records, but he already knew who made the call. And she wasn't quite the criminal mastermind that her late husband was.

CHAPTER THIRTY-SIX

Cameron sat on Roger's snowmobile and stared up at the frozen river that snaked in between the snowy peaks. He'd given her a quick tutorial on using the snowmobile, which was newer than Dane's. It had a heated seat, handlebars, and footrests. He'd also given her a map of the trails in the area and a stern warning to be careful.

Roger cautioned her of the dangers of traveling on the frozen river. Unlike a lake, he'd said, there could be areas where the ice thinned due to the moving water beneath it. He said this time of year it should be frozen solid, but if she hit a slushy or darkened patch not to trust it to hold her snowmobile.

She assured him she was meeting up with her old friend and would be perfectly fine. Which, she supposed, was somewhat true. She tucked the topographical map into her coat pocket and pulled down her helmet visor. Before she took off, Roger attached a coiled strap to her glove that ran to the ignition switch.

Cameron gave him a puzzled look.

"In case you somehow fall off," he explained," this strap connected to you will cut the engine immediately."

"Got it, right. Don't worry, Roger, I don't plan on falling off."

"No one ever does."

Even though it was after nine in the morning, the sun was just appearing behind the mountains to her right. Last night, she'd stayed up late studying a satellite map of the area using the hotel's Wi-Fi. With Dane's GPS and her map, she hoped to make it to Miles's cabin by late tomorrow afternoon. Once she was given the key to the snowmobile, she'd gone back to her plane and connected Dane's sled to the back, filled with supplies.

She squeezed the throttle with her right thumb, making the engine rev and the machine jump forward. Cameron eased her grip off the handle, and her body lurched forward before plopping down again on the warm seat.

She glanced behind her, making sure none of her supplies had spilled out of the sled. Taking a deep breath, she eased the throttle with a more gradual pressure. She sped down the river with increasing speed, enjoying the visceral sound that erupted from the motor in the sublime, isolated wilderness. She kept her mind focused on hunting the predator she'd come all this way for.

Cameron followed some older snowmobile tracks up the river. Over the last several miles, she'd gotten better at making the turns around the river bends. She spotted a big horn sheep running up the side of a mountain when she came around the corner, spooked by the drone of her motor.

She stopped and checked her GPS along with her map. She was within ten miles from where she would cut off through the mountains in the direction of Miles's cabin. Thinking of Miles, and John hiding out in his family's remote retreat, Cameron squeezed the throttle harder. She sped toward the next river bend and leaned left into the turn when she got closer.

The snowmobile's skis turned with her handlebars but lost traction atop the slick ice where the wind had blown the snow away. Instead of turning with the river, her snowmobile skidded sideways toward the bank. She leaned farther to the side and pulled down on the handlebars as hard as she could. The snowmobile continued to slide, and she let off the gas as the machine crashed into the side of rocky hillside. Cameron flew off the machine from the momentum of the collision and landed on the ice. Her helmet smacked against the frozen surface, and she slid on her belly until she came to a stop near the bank.

She rolled onto her back, breathing hard as she stared at the white sky. She got up slowly, surprised to not feel any injuries. She walked carefully on the slick surface toward her snowmobile up against the rocky cliff. It was still upright, and Cameron could only hope there hadn't been any serious damage.

She picked up the supplies that had toppled from her sled and resecured them inside. After climbing back onto the snowmobile, she reattached the toggle switch that was attached to her wrist.

"Guess it works," she said out loud.

She started the engine and gave it some gas. The engine revved, but the machine didn't move.

I can't fail at this.

She applied more pressure to the throttle, and the motor whirred even louder than before. She remembered the yellow reverse button Roger had shown her on the left handlebar. She pressed the button, tried the throttle again, and the machine soared backward with enough power that Cameron almost fell off again. She released the throttle, and the machine slowed to a stop. Somehow, the collision must have caused it to slip out of gear.

She sat back down and clicked the drive button, relieved when it powered up and she was once again pointed up the river. She went slower than before, knowing she couldn't afford any more accidents. Not if she was going to make it to John.

She eyed the color of the snow and ice as she cruised along. So far, it had all been the same color—an opaque white. She hadn't seen any slush or dark spots.

She felt the adrenaline from her crash subside as she took in the beautiful surroundings. She hadn't seen any other wildlife than the big horn sheep, but there was a peacefulness to the snow-capped peaks that protruded on both sides of the winding river. *No wonder John chose to spend the rest of his life here.*

The contrast between the snowy mountain valley and her Laurelhurst neighborhood made her feel a world away from her old life. How drastically everything had changed in the matter of a week. A few months ago, she'd pictured living in their Laurelhurst home for the rest of their lives. Growing old together.

She wondered what it would be like to see him again. After thinking she'd lost him forever and then learning he was never the man she thought he was. A monster.

She came to a corner and let up on the gas. She glanced at her speed, alarmed to see she was going over sixty miles per hour. Fortunately, this time her skis maintained traction during her turn. But when she rounded the curve, she was struck with terror at what lay ahead.

She opened her mouth to scream, but no sound came out. A large patch of dark moving water flowed beyond the ice less than fifty feet in front of her. At the speed she was going, there was no way she could slow down in time.

CHAPTER THIRTY-SEVEN

The patch of water looked about twenty feet across. If she braked, she would fall straight in. In a split-second decision, she closed her grip around the gas handle. She raced toward the flowing water and held her breath as the snowmobile skipped across the surface.

Cameron stood up on the footrests, preparing to jump off if it started to sink. But the snowmobile bounced atop the water and landed with a jolt as it hit the ice on the opposite side. Cameron didn't let up on the gas until she was sure she was on stable ice.

She stopped and turned back to look at the patch of free-flowing water, still in disbelief that she hadn't gone under. She couldn't see any supplies missing from inside her sled.

"Whoo!" she screamed into the silent wilderness.

It was the second time since she learned she'd been married to a sadistic serial killer that she felt like she'd cheated death. She pulled out Dane's GPS, along with her two maps. After studying her location, she looked at the hillside to her left.

She was within a mile from where she'd planned to veer off the river onto a groomed trail. But after seeing that patch of water, she was ready to get onto dry land. There was a large area bare of trees on the adjacent hillside, and she figured she could meet up with the groomed trail just over the ridge. She knew that eventually she needed to be able to handle the snowmobile in the deep powder of the mountains, anyway.

After planning her route, she zipped the maps and GPS back inside her pocket. She hit the gas and turned toward the mountain to her left.

She flew up the mountainside, afraid if she eased up on the gas that she might slide backward. By the time she reached the top, her arms felt like jelly from maneuvering the heavy machine through the deep snow.

She braked after she soared down the back of the hillside, fearful her speed would cause her to roll. She took her time, easing along the slope and dodging the occasional stump and evergreen that protruded from the white powder. When she reached the bottom, she met up with the groomed trail she'd seen on the map and sped along it across the small valley.

The trail ended before she got to the base of the next mountain. She continued until she found a clearing and stopped to take a drink from her thermos. As she withdrew a piece of moose jerky from its package, she thought of Dane killing that huge animal to save her. She replayed their final moment together in her mind as she bit off a piece of meat.

Dane was right. The smoky salt flavor was delicious. It was much better than the beef jerky she'd bought at her local organic market in Seattle.

She checked her watch. It would be dark in less than three hours, and she still needed to set up camp for the night. With her engine idling, she heard a sharp crack in the forest behind her. She turned, half-expecting to see John creeping up on her.

She lifted the visor on her helmet and scanned the sparse tree line to her left. Aside from a clump of snow falling from a pine branch, there was no movement. She checked behind her before she propelled up the mountainside. This one had more trees than the last, which kept her from going too fast as she zigzagged up the incline.

Her body felt weak from exhaustion when she reached the top, making her glad she'd eaten something when she stopped to take a drink. She'd had no idea driving a snowmobile would take so much energy. She planned to rest on the ridge before heading down, but the mountain peaked with a sharp edge, leaving nowhere level enough to stop.

The front of her snowmobile lifted into the air when Cameron crested the ridge. She felt weightless before she was pulled forward from the momentum of the machine soaring down the back of the mountain. She pushed against the handlebars to keep from going over the front when it made impact with the steep slope.

White powder erupted from beneath her, clouding her vision as she zoomed down the ridge. She felt for the brake and squeezed, thankful there were barely any trees on this side. The snowmobile slowed, and she turned as the rear slid sideways atop the soft snow.

The powder settled and Cameron moved slowly down the cliffside as her visibility cleared. She had nearly caught her breath when she watched the smooth white surface crack like a hard-boiled egg seconds before a wave appeared to roll beneath the snow. There was a thunderous boom behind her as the snow broke away from the slope.

CHAPTER THIRTY-EIGHT

Cameron had never seen an avalanche before, but there was no mistaking what was happening. Mounds of snow plunged down the mountainside on either side of her. The snow beneath the back of her snowmobile crumbled.

Her snowmobile tilted backward as the snow separated from the ground. Cameron squeezed the throttle and soared down the steep cliff. Snow cascaded down the mountain all around her, and she kept her grip clenched around the throttle as she fought to maintain control. She veered to the side toward smooth snow, not seeing the cracks until she sped over them.

Another thunder-like crack erupted from the mountain. Cameron zigzagged down the steep decline, avoiding the thick patch of evergreens to her right. She was tempted to turn around and look but forced herself to focus—she had to get out of the way of the wall of snow. After turning to the left, she spun around to check if she was finally out of danger. The huge pile of snow was still crashing down the mountain, but she'd managed to move out of its path.

She turned too sharp, sending her tumbling off the snowmobile as the machine tipped onto its side. She landed on her back and sailed headfirst toward the bottom. Hyperventilating, she stared at her feet sliding down the mountain at a terrifying speed.

"Ughh!" Her momentum ceased when she impacted with the snow pile at the base of the mountain, knocking the air from her lungs.

She wheezed when she sucked in a hard breath. She knew she should get up and run to make sure she was clear of any more snowfall. But she could only manage to breathe in and out as she stared at the patchy afternoon sky.

After a few minutes, she managed to sit up. She spotted her red snowmobile on its side atop a mound of snow about thirty feet away from her. Thankfully, the sled was still attached to the back.

She grunted as she brushed the snow off her body and stood. Before she dared to move, she scanned the cliffside for moving snow.

She had no idea how likely it was that another avalanche would occur. *Was an aftershock a thing with avalanches like with earthquakes?* She kept her eyes on the surrounding slope as she trekked toward her snowmobile.

Her feet sank knee deep into the snow as she struggled to get to the machine. She was out of breath and shaking from the adrenaline rush when she reached the top of the mound.

Cameron examined the hillside another time before she gripped the handlebars and leaned back, straining to right the snowmobile atop the soft snow. When it didn't budge, Cameron let go and found Dane's snow shovel inside the sled. She dug beside the snowmobile, clearing the snow from its side and out of the track.

She stuck the shovel into the snow before she gripped the handlebars and pulled the heavy machine toward her a second time. Despite the subzero temperature, Cameron felt sweat drip between her breasts. This time, the snowmobile yielded to her weight.

Cameron lost her balance when the machine lifted upright. She let go of the handlebars so she didn't pull it on top of her as she rolled down the mound. A throaty snarl broke the quiet of the valley.

Cameron sat up with a jolt and stared at the tree line straight ahead. The snarl sounded again, and she jumped to her feet. A large black wolf emerged from the trees.

Its yellow eyes bore into hers. Cameron stood still, remembering what Valerie said about maintaining eye contact, afraid to move or turn her eyes away. The wolf lowered its head and growled, opening its mouth wide enough for Cameron to see its long white fangs. The wolf took a step toward her and as if on cue a pack of grey and white wolves appeared in the forest behind it. They were just like the wolf in her motel room. Except alive. Their eyes glowed in the shadows, and every pair of them was focused on Cameron.

Without taking her eyes off the leader, Cameron felt for the key attached to the safety strap that was still clipped to her wrist. The black wolf bared its teeth again with a vicious growl. There was anguish in the animal's snarl as it morphed into a high-pitched sound. Once she had the key in her grip, she bolted for the snowmobile at the top of the mound.

Cameron's legs sank into the soft snow as she frantically ran toward her snowmobile. Out of the corner of her eye, she could see the dark blur of the leader silently sprinting across the valley straight for her, with its pack following behind.

She pulled her legs out of the snow, willing them to move faster. When she got to the top, she threw herself onto the snowmobile. The black wolf leapt onto the base of the snow pile, leaving her no time to process how it had covered the distance so fast.

Her hand shook as she fumbled to get the key into the ignition.

"Come on!"

It slid inside the hole on her second try. *Please start. Please start.* The wolf lunged at her leg when she pressed the push start button on the left handlebar.

A sharp snap reverberated from the force of its jaw as its teeth sunk into her pant leg. The engine roared to life. The wolf sneered and tore off a piece of her snow pants. It retreated from the noise as Cameron squeezed the throttle and flew down the mound, landing with a bounce on the valley floor.

She turned to the right and sped between the thinning trees. Her heart thumped against her chest. She waited until she reached a speed of forty-five to turn around. The pack stood still, watching her from the base of the mountain. She exhaled when she turned back and focused on maneuvering through the valley as fast as was safely possible. She continued north for another hour before she stopped to set up camp.

CHAPTER THIRTY-NINE

Cameron turned off her snowmobile and sat in silence, scanning the surrounding trees for signs of life before dismounting. She checked her GPS against her topographical map in the fading light. She was less than twenty miles from the cabin. Tomorrow, she'd have to go up and over one more mountain, larger but less steep than the last one she'd crossed. She could only hope there wouldn't be another avalanche.

She checked her leg beneath her ripped snow pant, glad to see the wolf hadn't broken her skin. There was an eerie stillness to the forest after she'd gotten used to the drone from the snowmobile's powerful engine. After gliding across the snow at the speed of a car, her movements felt slow and clumsy when she climbed off the snowmobile. She went to the sled to retrieve the snow shovel and remembered she'd left it behind at the base of the mountain.

She eyed the large bins in the back of the sled, along with Dane's hunting rifle. At least she'd kept the rest of her supplies. She stomped the snow with her boots before laying the firewood she'd bought in Eagle on the ground.

According to Valerie's book, wolves were afraid of fire and smoke. Cameron hoped it would be enough to deter them. She also felt chilled to the core from her exertion and the drop in temperature from the sun moving below the mountains.

She crumpled the newspaper she'd taken from her hotel, glad to see that there was at least one paper in the world where the serial killer and his wife didn't feature. She lit the paper with a lighter. She stood over the growing flames, allowing the heat to permeate through her winter outer gear before she set up the tent.

She bit off a piece of moose jerky from its wrapper. *Dane must know by now who I really am.* She pushed his face from her mind, not wanting to dwell on what he must think of her.

She struggled to set up his ice fishing shack beside the fire, which took her three times as long as it had taken him. Once the shack was standing, she unfolded the cot and slid it inside, along with Dane's subzero sleeping bag and the propane heater along with two bottles of fuel.

The forest was dark when she stepped outside by the fire. She added another log, still in awe that it could burn atop the snow. She crouched down. An overwhelming sense of loneliness encompassed her as she felt the warmth from the flames against her face. Other than Simon, she had no one.

She pulled another piece of moose jerky from the bag when she felt rain drops on her nose. She looked up, knowing it was too cold for it to be raining. The drops came down harder from the pine branches overhead. They sizzled as they landed atop the flames.

She cursed herself for being so stupid.

Her fire was melting the snow off the branches. She used a fresh piece of firewood to spread out the burning logs and then she threw snow on the fire. *It's time for bed, anyway.* She glanced at the tent, which was just beyond reach of the dripping water.

She took her bag of jerky and thermos and went inside the tent. As she was about to zip close the door, light from the sky caught her eye. Now that the flames had dimmed, the sky was streaked with an unnatural shade of bright green. It was breathtaking.

She stared in wonder until she heard a wolf howl in the distance. She zipped the tent and crawled inside the down sleeping bag after removing her outerwear. Once she was completely cocooned, aside from her face, she closed her eyes.

She felt the energy drain from her body as she listened to the distant howls and breathed in the scent of Dane's aftershave. It was hard to imagine how close she was to John. A few months ago, she would have given anything to see him again. Now, she'd risk everything to know he'd taken his last breath.

Eventually, she gave into her exhaustion and slept deeper than she had in months.

CHAPTER FORTY

Cameron woke before the sun. She checked her watch and saw it was just after six. She had nearly two hours until daylight. She stayed inside the warmth of Dane's sleeping bag until seven, using the flashlight to plot her course on the map.

She'd leave as soon as it was light and would use Dane's snowshoes to walk the last two miles to the cabin. It was farther away than she'd planned, but the wind was coming from the south, which would carry the sound of her snowmobile toward the cabin. She hoped to be there by early afternoon.

After pulling on her boots and coat, she stepped outside into the subzero morning air. She made another fire, this time making sure it wasn't under a tree. All of her drink bottles were frozen inside the sled, so she boiled snow and dropped a bottle of Gatorade into the pot to thaw it.

After she drank it, she did the same with a bottle of water and poured the warm liquid into her thermos. She ate a protein bar by the fire before putting on a headlamp to take down the shack. She hadn't heard any wolves since she'd woken that morning, but she looked around periodically for any sign of them.

By first light, she had all the camping gear loaded back into the sled. Large snowflakes fell when she topped up her gas tank with the extra fuel she'd brought. She climbed onto the snowmobile and pulled on her helmet. The engine reverberated through her quiet surroundings when she started it up and she squeezed the throttle.

She sped past the dwindling fire and headed toward the base of the mountain to the left of the valley. She could hardly believe she'd made it this far. This was it.

A shiver travelled down her arms as she steeled herself for what she was about to do. There was no turning back now. She raced up the mountainside, careful to dodge the occasional evergreens and boulders. *I'm coming for you, baby.*

Cameron idled the snowmobile at the base of the other side of the mountain and checked her GPS. She'd made it up and over without incident—or avalanche. The cabin was ten miles north. She checked her compass before steering toward the forested area up ahead.

After eight miles, she killed the engine. She pulled off her helmet and listened for signs of life. But the forest was unnervingly silent. She retrieved Dane's snowshoes from the sled and strapped them onto her boots.

She grabbed his hunting rifle, ejected the magazine, and inserted two cartridges from Dane's ammo box. After sliding the full clip back into the rifle, she lifted the bolt action and pulled it toward her to chamber a round. She flicked on the safety before slinging it over her shoulder.

She put the small flashlight and zip ties in her pocket. She decided not to use Dane's handcuffs when she found the zip ties among his camping gear. If John's body was ever found, she didn't want anything to lead back to Dane.

She forced herself to have another protein bar, even though she felt too nervous to eat. She took a large drink from her thermos and laid it inside the sled before checking her GPS one more time.

She sifted through her bin of supplies and removed the bag housing the sleeping bag. She slipped Roger's custom bear trap inside and slipped it over her other shoulder. It was heavy, but she would manage.

She kept her compass in her gloved palm and she trudged west through the forest, aware of every little sound she made. It was crucial that she maintain the element of surprise.

She stopped halfway to catch her breath and focus her thoughts. Her anxiety was building the closer she got to John and interfering with her ability to think clearly, but she urged herself on. *You've done this before.*

She continued the last mile to his cabin, stepping as quietly as possible on the soft snow. When she got within a few hundred yards, she found footprints on the ground. *John's.*

She looked around and stepped behind a large tree to unstrap her snowshoes. She turned off the safety on Dane's hunting rifle and aimed the gun out front as she moved through the trees. She smelled smoke and knew she was getting close.

She crept forward until a log cabin came into her view inside a small clearing. Firewood was stacked high against the side. Smoke blew from a chimney at the top of the roofline. Beside it, a snowmobile was parked beneath a covering.

Her breath caught in her throat as she looked through the window and saw the silhouette of a man. She tucked behind the closest tree and exhaled through her mouth. Even though she only saw him for a split second, she recognized the confident way John moved.

She lifted the sleeve of her coat and glanced at her watch. She'd made good time. It was almost three. She slid the bag off her shoulder and stretched her aching back muscles before turning her jacket inside out, exposing the white liner before she pulled it back on.

After pressing her back against the tree trunk, she withdrew the heavy bear trap. She peered around the tree at the cabin. John had moved away from the window.

Crouching down, she ran toward the cabin, bear trap in hand. She didn't slow down until she reached the exterior wall. She moved on her hands and knees toward the bottom of the porch, dragging the trap beside her.

After sweeping away the layer of fresh powder, she positioned the bear trap on the ground in front of the lowest step. She opened it the way Roger had shown her, cringing when it locked into place with a metallic clack, then covered it with snow. She worked to quiet her breathing as she slid the rifle strap off her shoulder and tucked the gun under her arm.

She stood up halfway and stepped over the trap before climbing the steps. The front door was solid wood. Using her teeth, she tugged off her left-hand glove and reached for the front doorknob. It turned silently in her grip.

Without a moment's hesitation, Cameron flung the door open wide and stepped inside, gun barrel first.

Flames flickered from the fireplace and filled the cabin with warmth. A bearded man whipped around at the kitchen sink, his wide eyes startled by the intrusion. There was no light aside from the fire and the light coming through the windows. But there was no mistaking his face. And the evil in his hazel eyes.

Staring at him, she was sure now it had always been there. She'd just been too blind to see it.

His mouth fell open. "Cameron?"

She lifted the rifle and put his forehead in her sights. "Hello, John. You left without saying goodbye."

CHAPTER FORTY-ONE

Tanner paused the video and rubbed his eyes. He'd been going over the red-light camera footage closest to Cameron's home for over three hours from the night Alicia Lopez and Olivia Rossi went missing. He guessed she had driven back from the cabin after dark, which made it too difficult to spot her Lexus on the weather webcam heading to Seattle on Snoqualmie Pass.

Washington state law prohibited the red-light footage from being admissible for anything other than a traffic violation. But if he could find her behind the wheel at a certain time, he might be able to find her on another traffic camera that he could use as evidence.

He pressed play and stared at the dark intersection. The timestamp on the footage was 2:25 a.m. He fast forwarded until a set of headlights came into view. He played the footage at normal speed and tapped the screen to pause it when the white car entered the intersection.

He leaned closer to the screen, recognizing Cameron's license plate immediately. His pulse quickened.

"Mulholland, have you finished that paperwork I need for the Newburg case?"

Tanner enlarged the screen, vaguely aware of his sergeant standing over his cubicle. His jaw fell open as he recognized the grainy image of the person behind the wheel.

"Mulholland!"

He waved his hand in the air, not bothering to look up from his screen. "Sorry, not now." He stared at the frozen image, blown away by what he saw. He'd been wrong this whole time. He typed a name into his keyboard and found the address he was looking for. He checked the time and pulled out his phone.

"I need those forms filled out." His sergeant's tone was gruff.

Tanner ignored him and stood from his chair.

"Hey! Did you hear me, Mulholland?"

"They'll be on your desk in the morning!" Tanner called as he raced down the hallway of the Homicide Unit.

CHAPTER FORTY-TWO

John put his palms in the air.

"Cameron...." His voice was calm, placating.

Now that he'd recovered from the shock of seeing her, he was attempting to regain control of the situation.

He looked out the window and then back at her. "How'd you get here?"

Cameron kept the barrel aimed at his forehead.

"Baby, let's talk. Put that away. I can explain."

She kept her finger on the trigger. "I'm not here to talk."

Keeping his hands in the air, he took a step toward her. "Don't move!"

"All right. Easy." He slowly lowered his hands. "How did you—"

"Find you? It wasn't that hard."

"This isn't what it looks like." He took another step.

"Stop!"

"Sweetheart, you have to believe me." She recognized the tone he used to sway juries. "The cops were going to falsely accuse me of being The Teacher Killer. I had no other choice."

"You *are* The Teacher Killer. I found the photos. At your cabin."

His lips curled into a dark smile. "Ah." He sighed.

His eyes traveled to the side of the room. Cameron's followed. John lunged toward her and closed his hand around the barrel of her rifle. She squeezed the trigger as he forced the end of the gun toward the ceiling. The blast echoed in the small space. Wood chips fell from the bullet that had struck the exposed logs above them.

Cameron went to chamber another round as John wrapped his arms around her waist, knocking her to the ground. John quickly crawled away after her back slammed against the floor. She yanked the bolt handle back, ejecting the spent round. The shell casing clamored to the floor as John reached for a shotgun that leaned against the wall.

She slid the bolt handle forward, aimed her gun at his leg, and fired. John cried out in pain. Cameron swallowed back her disgust at the pitiful whimper that escaped his mouth after all that he'd inflicted on others. She crawled across the floor and kicked the gun out of his reach.

His hand clenched around her ankle. She chambered a new round and pointed the barrel at his face. "Let go."

He stared at her. "What are you going to do? Kill me like you killed Miles? You're no better than me," he seethed through clenched teeth.

She was afraid he would try another attack and she'd have to shoot him. And he couldn't get off that easy. After a moment, he released her leg from his grip.

"I'm nothing like you." She pulled her foot away and stood. "Get up, John."

He grimaced and glanced at the blood seeping from his pant leg. "I can't."

Cameron adjusted the aim of her gun. "Maybe it will be easier if I put a bullet in your other leg."

He let out an obnoxious grunt and winced as he struggled to stand. Cameron picked his gun up off the floor and slid the strap over her left shoulder.

She took a step back. "Get outside."

"I don't have any shoes on." He motioned to his socks. "What are you planning to do? Take me back?"

"I'm not taking you back. Just go. You won't need shoes."

He smirked and stepped toward the open doorway, seeming to forget the bullet in his thigh. "You got the police out here or something, Cameron? Or are you going to kill me by frostbite?"

She thrust the barrel into his back. "Move!"

He stepped onto the porch. "You know, Cameron. I never thought I'd see you again. You look good as a redhead—more beautiful than ever." He looked around. "How did you get here all by yourself?"

Cameron followed behind him. "Down the steps, John."

He shot her a look over his shoulder. "You're quite a woman. I've always known that. But you don't know these woods like I do. There's a lot of dangers out there. You may not make it back alive to wherever you came from. Why don't you stay here with me? You know I've always loved you, right?"

"John, go."

He did as instructed, crying out like a child when he put weight on the leg she'd shot. He stepped off the porch and Cameron heard the metallic clash of the trap close around his ankle.

"Ahhh!" He threw his hands at the trap as he fell onto the snow.

Cameron squeezed the trigger, sending a bullet into his upper arm. John cried out again.

"You bitch!" he managed to scream, as he writhed in pain on the frozen ground.

As soon as the bullet entered his arm, Cameron pulled the zip ties from her pocket and flew down the steps. With a knee on John's back, she secured the ties around both of his wrists from behind.

He thrashed beneath her, and Cameron fell onto the snow beside him. She rolled out of reach of his flailing form.

"What the—ahh!" He glared at her with gritted teeth.

Cameron stood and placed her hands on her knees as she watched John's blood spill onto the white snow. She let him squirm and yell for a few minutes, letting the energy drain from his body.

When his movements slowed, she grabbed him beneath the armpits. He fought against her, but it wasn't enough to stop her from dragging him slowly away from the cabin. She took two breaks to catch her breath before she managed to pull him to the base of a nearby tree.

Daylight was beginning to wane from the grey sky when she retrieved the rope from the tent bag. John fell to his side onto the snow when Cameron wrapped the first loop around him. She secured the rope behind the tree and pushed his upper body against the tree trunk before tying another loop. He bit her hand when she fed the rope between his arm and his torso.

"Ahh!" She tried to pull away as he fought to free his hands from the ties.

She shook her arm in a frantic motion and fell onto the ground when she finally pulled it away from John's mouth. He spit her glove onto the snow as she rested her throbbing hand against her chest. Her glove had kept his teeth from breaking her skin, but it hurt like hell.

She pushed herself to her feet using her other hand. "I know you killed that girl in Tok."

He stared at her. "What girl?"

She grabbed the rope and tossed it across his body. "You know you're dying to admit it. You sick bastard."

"Bethany?"

Cameron's stomach rolled hearing her name on John's tongue.

"She was a little young for my taste," he continued, "but, in a town that small, pickings were slim. And she reminded me of someone."

She moved around the tree before grabbing the ends and pulling them taut. She hadn't expected John to be remorseful.

But hearing him speak so flippantly about taking Bethany's life fueled her rage. She wouldn't waste her breath telling him about Grace. She wouldn't give him the satisfaction.

"How can you not even feel an ounce of remorse?"

He grunted as Cameron tied the rope into a tight knot. "You know I made it look like you helped me kill those women, right? Mulholland won't stop digging—he's a persistent son of a bitch. And the investigation is going to point directly to you. If you go back to Seattle, you'll be going to jail. And then there's poor, poor Miles."

John writhed in pain as Cameron moved around the tree to face him. The color had drained from his face. She hoped he didn't pass out from blood loss too soon.

"Cam, stay here. With me." The fake charisma had returned to his voice. "We can be free. Together. We're both killers. That's why I picked you."

Picked me. His words made her sick.

A wolf howled from beyond the trees.

"The wolves are out John. Hunting time." She picked her glove off the snow and pulled it on. "Did you know there have been rumors of rabid wolves in this area? And do you know what that makes them do?"

Beads of sweat had formed on John's forehead. He gritted his teeth. He started to bend his leg not ensnared in the bear trap but winced before resting it back onto the bloodstained snow. Cameron moved around the back of the tree and tied another knot in the rope.

"How do you know I killed Bethany?"

"Just a hunch. I looked through your hunting magazines and remembered you always dreamed of living off grid in Alaska. Then I read she was studying to be an English teacher and bore a striking resemblance to the first woman you killed."

"I figured it wouldn't be long before Mulholland linked me to the Teacher Killings, but I didn't expect you to become Nancy Drew." He let out a sharp cry of pain as blood oozed from the bullet hole in his thigh. "*Shit!* Why did you come after me?" John asked. "Why couldn't you just let it go? I never hurt *you*."

Cameron withdrew the wolf howler from her pack and stepped around the tree in front of John before putting it to her lips. She blew into the mouthpiece. No sound came out. She shook the call and tried again. Still nothing. *It could have broken when I crashed on the river. The gear flew everywhere.*

She threw it into the snow and drew in a deep breath. She closed her eyes, lifted her chin, and howled as loudly as her lungs would allow.

"What the hell are you doing, Cameron?" There was panic for the first time in John's voice. "If you're going to kill me just do it!"

"Not yet, John." She howled again. Her call resonated through the white woods.

"Cameron! Let me go!"

A wolf howled its reply in the distance.

Cameron howled a third time.

John swore and tried to stand, but she'd tied him too tightly for him to even slide down the tree.

"Or just shoot me already! Isn't that what you came here for?" John glared up at her. There was no hiding the hatred in his eyes. "You're a killer, Cam. We're the same. You think you're better than me, but you're not."

"I'm nothing like you. And I'm not going to kill you, John. You're already dead." Cameron squatted down so that she and John were eye-to-eye. "You were mauled to death by a wild animal, right?"

Wolves howled in unison beyond the trees. They had already moved in closer since she made the first call.

"You hear that, John? You're going to wish you died from a bear attack by the time they're through. Do you know the difference between being attacked by a bear and a pack of wolves? Come on, you're a big hunter."

John grunted as he worked to free his hands behind his back.

"I'll tell you. Bears kill their prey by delivering an instantly fatal wound to the head or the neck. Wolves kill by attrition. I had to look that word up. They kill as a pack, biting away at the legs, groin, and gut until their prey collapses from exhaustion and pain. Then—and this is the worst part, I think—they go to work devouring their victim's flesh, leaving them alive for an excruciating period before they finally die."

"Ahhh!" John thrashed beneath the rope.

Cameron stood. "You're only going to draw them in quicker if you scream."

"Cameron! Please. *Please.* Don't do this. I'm so sorry." A whimper escaped his throat, and tears welled in his eyes.

Tears for himself.

John turned toward the sound of another howl. They were getting closer. She had to go.

"This is your doing, John."

He screamed her name as she walked toward the cabin. She didn't have much time, but she wanted to see how John had possibly been living up here. She felt the heat from the fireplace when she stepped inside. The small space was reminiscent of their Cle Elum cabin, only more rustic.

She ran her hand along a bear hide that hung from the wall and recognized a leather-bound Jack London novel on the couch. She moved toward a bookshelf beside the fireplace, which was neatly organized with classic literature. She skimmed the faded titles on the spines. *Fitzgerald. Hemingway. Steinbeck. Salinger.*

She turned from the bookshelf, feeling sick knowing how much John had enjoyed living out his off-grid fantasy. While his victims would never take another breath, John was basking in his ultimate freedom.

"Cameron!"

She ignored his cries from outside and moved toward the kitchen. There was a small wood stove beside the sink, but no fridge. Canned foods were stacked atop the back of the counter. *Had John been prepping this place during his Alaskan hunting trips?* She stopped when she spotted a satellite phone on the wood counter. It was exactly like Dane's.

Who could John possibly have to call?

A chorus of howls echoed through the open cabin door. She couldn't stay any longer. She swiped the phone off the counter and slid it into her pocket.

A log crackled from the fireplace. Cameron stopped in the middle of the cabin, tempted to set it on fire. But she continued toward the door, knowing the flames—and smoke—would scare off the wolves.

She saw movement on the top of the closest ridge when she got outside. It looked like the same wolf pack that had tried to attack her yesterday. Above them, a waxing moon had appeared in the sky.

"Cameron!" John grunted from the base of the tree as he tried to break away from his restraints.

She felt his phone in her pocket as she marched toward him. She debated asking him what he had used it for but decided not to waste her breath. She could look at the call history when she was safely out of these woods.

But there was one thing she wanted to know. John's hairline was wet with perspiration when she stood in front of him.

"What did you use your life insurance money for? The fifty grand."

"A plane." He grunted. "I paid cash and had it stored at a guy's hangar in Idaho until I needed it to get out of the Frank Church Wilderness."

"Goodbye, John."

Cameron moved around the tree.

John flailed beneath the rope. "Cameron! Come on...I'll give you the money, everything. You will never, ever hear from me again. No one will. I promise."

"Won't hear from you again? I have to say that looks taken care of."

She lifted the tent bag, which felt light without the bear trap. She shot a wary glance over her shoulder at the wolves descending the nearby hillside. After strapping on Dane's snowshoes, she took a drink from her thermos and pulled out a large piece of jerky to eat while she hiked. She would have to hurry to make it back to her snowmobile by dark—and stay ahead of the wolves. Although, she hoped they would be too busy with John to come for her.

John continued to scream her name. She pulled her hood over her head and trekked through the snow.

CHAPTER FORTY-THREE

Gina Castelli opened the front door of her three-story brick mansion in Capitol Hill. Tanner immediately caught a strong whiff of her perfume. He recognized Simon's wife from her driver's license photo. Her sleek black bob framed her round face. She wore a fitted maroon sweatsuit.

"Gina Castelli?"

She looked Tanner up and down. "Yes. Can I help you?"

He flashed a disarming smile. "I'm Detective Tanner Mulholland from the Seattle Homicide Unit. Could I come in?"

"Oh. Simon isn't home. He's still at the office." She started to close the door.

"I actually wanted to speak to you, if I could."

Her eyebrows knitted together.

"I just have a few questions," he added. "About Cameron Prescott."

She hesitated in the half-open doorway. Tanner held his breath.

"Oh. Okay. Sure."

She opened the door wide, and Tanner let out an internal sigh. She led him past a white pillar in the pre-war home's grand foyer and into a sitting room with a marble fireplace. She motioned to a red leather couch.

"Please, have a seat."

"Thank you."

She sat in an armchair to his right. Tanner tried not to show his relief that she'd let him inside as he gazed out at Lake Union through the window behind her. She turned to follow his stare.

"Beautiful, isn't it?"

He nodded. "Very." He looked around the room. The nearly one-hundred-year-old home looked brand new.

"We're in the process of renovating the entire home," she said. She pointed to the crown molding. "We're keeping some of the original features though."

"It looks great. The whole home?" It was large, even for Capitol Hill. "That sounds like quite a project." *And costly.*

"Yes. We started a few months ago, and we're doing one floor at a time. We just finished this main level, and the upstairs is completely torn up."

"How long have you lived here?"

"Twenty years." She frowned. "I should probably call Simon and let him know you're here." She grabbed her phone from the end table beside her but looked at Tanner instead of making the call. "I thought I'd see him more after John passed away, but now he's consumed with helping Cameron." She picked a fuzz off her sleeve. When she looked up, her frown disappeared. "So, what did you need to know about her?"

"Did you see her on the night of June 19, the summer before last?"

She pressed her lips together. "The night those teachers went missing?"

She'd been following the news. Or Simon had been keeping her up to date. "Yes."

"We went out for dinner. Downtown."

"You and Simon?"

She shook her head. "No…Cameron and I."

Tanner couldn't hide his surprise. Why hadn't Simon told him if he'd known Cameron had an alibi for at least part of the night? It was all starting to make sense.

"I didn't see any charge from that night on Cameron's credit cards."

Tanner noticed her change in posture.

"You've done your homework, detective." She waved a finger toward her chest. "I paid. Simon was the one who insisted I take her out. She and I never socialized much, but John was worried about Cameron spending so much time alone when he was out of town. We left the restaurant in plenty of time for her to…." She clamped her lips shut.

"What time did you leave the restaurant?"

"I can't remember exactly. Between seven and eight. Cameron had said she was tired. She's a homebody, that one."

"And did she drive to the restaurant?"

"No, I picked her up."

"Do you remember what Simon was doing that evening?"

She shifted again in her chair and ran a finger across the back of her phone. "Working late. As usual."

He didn't miss the marked bitterness in her tone.

"What time did he come home that night?"

"I thought this was about Cameron."

Tanner gave her another moment to respond. She didn't.

"Was Simon here when you got home from having dinner with Cameron?"

"No. He came home after I'd gone to bed. He was preparing for some big case out of town. I don't think I saw him much that weekend." She shrugged her shoulders.

"Where did he go? Where was the meeting?"

"I'm not sure. I only remember because he borrowed my car."

Tanner worked to keep his facial expression neutral.

"Oh, I remember." She leaned forward in her chair. "He went to check out some property in the mountains. He didn't want to take his Bentley since he'd just gotten it. So, he took my Range Rover." She scoffed. "Good thing he doesn't buy me as nice of car as he gets for himself."

"Do you remember when he came home?"

Her eyes traced the ornate molding as she pondered the question. "I don't remember if he even came home that night, Detective Mulholland."

Tanner stood and took a couple steps toward the door. "Thank you." He needed to get back to the office and go through the traffic footage. "I really appreciate your time."

The detective's sudden departure took her off guard. "Do you think Cameron was helping John?"

"I'm sorry, but I can't answer that. Thank you again. I'll let myself out. And once again, lovely home."

CHAPTER FORTY-FOUR

Cameron marched through the deep snow as quickly as her body would allow. She'd been walking for over half an hour. She should be halfway back to her snowmobile. Twilight had settled over the forest. John's screams had faded and morphed into cries of agony that she could now barely hear. The howling had stopped. *Mealtime.*

She forced herself not to dwell on it. She had to save her energy for finding her snowmobile and setting up camp. There would be plenty of time to reflect on this day later.

When she last checked her GPS, it was nearly dead. She turned it off to preserve the battery, hoping it would have enough juice for her to turn it on one more time. The fresh snow had made it impossible for her to follow the tracks she'd made earlier.

The temperature had dropped significantly with the setting sun. She longed for the warmth of the snowmobile's heated seat as she commanded her legs to keep going. She glanced at her compass and continued southeast. Her boots felt like they were filled with lead as she struggled to lift the snowshoes, one after the other.

It was nearly dark when she stopped to check her GPS. She pressed the power button with her gloved hand and worried it was already dead as she waited for it to turn on.

"Come on. Please work."

The screen lit up. A low battery signal flashed in the upper right corner. A triangle showed her location about two thousand feet northwest from where she'd left the snowmobile.

"Thank God."

She exhaled and the screen went dark. The words *shutting down* appeared over the dark background before it turned off.

"Great."

She'd left the charger in the sled with the rest of gear. Hopefully, with the compass, she would find it. *You're not far,* she told herself. She couldn't allow herself to think about how long she could survive wandering out here in the night. The temperature would drop another fifteen degrees as the night went on; she doubted she would make it until morning. She dropped the GPS back inside the pack and pulled out the flashlight.

She shined the light on the compass and moved southeast. *Just a little farther.* Minutes later, it was completely dark.

She paused beside a large tree. She pulled the last strip of jerky from its pack, hoping the protein would give her energy to make it the final way. But as she bit into the meat, she felt too tired to even chew. *I should just sit down for a minute.*

She sank beside the tree, thinking how good it felt to rest. She leaned her head against the rough, frozen trunk and closed her eyes.

An owl hooted from the branches above, making it even more peaceful.

"Get up." Cameron jerked her head upright, instructing herself to rise. She knew that if she didn't get up now, she never would. She'd freeze to death in minutes.

In slow motion, she pushed herself to her feet. She held out her arm and moved the flashlight back and forth across the tree line. A flash of red caught her eye. She stopped and swung the flashlight back in its direction.

She crossed the last few yards to the snowmobile as fast as her depleted body allowed. She let it idle after starting the ignition, feeling herself revive from the warmth of its heated seat and handlebars. After plugging the GPS into its remote charger, she forced herself to drink what was left in her thermos and put two protein bars into her pockets to thaw while she drove back to the campsite.

She took it slow over the ridge in the dark. When she reached the base of the ridge, near where she had camped the night before, the sky was lit up by the northern lights. For a second or two, she pictured John tied to the tree, now that the wolves had their turn at him.

After building a fire, she basked in its heat while she ate her protein bars and mustered enough energy to set up the shack. She filled her thermos with boiling water and left the fire going as she kicked off her boots and climbed inside.

With the heater going, she huddled inside Dane's sleeping bag and closed her eyes. The wilderness was quiet, aside from the crackling fire. It struck her how close she was to giving up when she'd been only a stone's throw from the snowmobile.

She rolled onto her side and opened her eyes. Seeing John today had been like seeing a total stranger. How quickly the evil came into his eyes when he saw her.

Remembering the satellite phone, she unzipped the sleeping bag and pulled it out of her coat pocket. There was no passcode, and Cameron used the buttons below the small screen to find the call log. There were several calls to the same number—a Seattle area code—but no name was listed.

She returned to the menu and found the messages icon, but there were no texts stored on the phone. She'd have to wait until she could check her phone to verify who John was calling, but she could guess.

But why? She zipped herself back inside the warmth of Dane's sleeping bag and reflected on what it could mean. Endless scenarios filled her mind but none that made any sense. After the day she'd had, it would be better to rest. She was just grasping at straws as exhausted as she was.

She wondered how likely it was that John's remains would ever be discovered. She contemplated going back in the morning and removing his teeth—just in case. She wasn't sure what she'd use to extract them, but there would probably be a tool inside the cabin that would do the job. Although, Mulholland already had John's DNA. So, if John was found, his teeth wouldn't make a difference. And she had no desire to see John's ravaged remains. Imaging them was enough.

She closed her eyes and remembered dancing with John at their wedding. He sang off key to every song as they'd cruised Lake Washington on a rented yacht. He'd looked impeccable in his white tuxedo. She'd been so in love with him. She knew in that moment that, with him by her side, everything was going to be okay.

She forced the memory from her mind and wondered again about John's final moments.

CHAPTER FORTY-FIVE

Cameron lifted her Cessna off the Eagle airstrip, glad to leave the snowy wilderness—and John—behind. She'd slept through the night in Dane's ice shack and woken with a fresh resolve to conquer the return journey. After she made it back to Eagle, she decided to use the remaining two hours of daylight to start her trip home.

She followed the Yukon River south, replaying her moments with her husband in her mind.

She'd been tempted to fly over his cabin. Try to see what was left of him and make sure he was dead. But she decided to leave him in the past, where he belonged. No matter what happened now, she would always have the peace that John was dead.

She looked right out the side window toward Tok. Dane would likely know who she really was by now. She would hate to know what he must think of her.

She continued southeast and crossed the Canadian border with the river. *Would Mulholland be waiting to arrest me when I get back?* She thought of Simon. Cameron turned on her phone, holding her breath as it powered up. She didn't bother looking up the number on John's satellite phone again—she'd know it when she saw it.

She opened her recent calls and felt a familiar stab of betrayal. *Was there no one in her life she could trust?* John had been calling Simon every week since his disappearance.

Why would he help John get away with this? What else had he helped John do?

CHAPTER FORTY-SIX

Two days later, Cameron opened her front door and Simon pushed past her before she had a chance to invite him in. She'd called him less than an hour ago to tell him she was home. She spotted the Parkers peering at them from under their porch lights across the street.

"I don't even have words for you right now." He paced atop the hardwood floor of her entryway.

I could say the same, she thought. From his suit, Cameron guessed he'd come straight from the office.

"You might as well have gone on TV and announced you were John's accomplice. How could you not see how running away like that would look?" He stopped, making eye contact with her for the first time. He raised a flattened palm toward her hair, as if pointing at key evidence in court. "And what is this? A *disguise?*" He put both hands on top of his own head and turned around. He blew out a breath and stared into her living room. "Oh, Cameron."

She followed his gaze. The room didn't look the same without the baby grand, but this was no time to dwell on it.

"Why don't you have a seat?" She moved past him and sank into her favorite velvet chair.

She waited in silence before he complied. She watched him closely as he sat down across from her. This was John's oldest friend.

He crossed his leg, reminding her of the morning he'd come over after she had learned the truth about John. "You know, we could've had a strong defense before you ran off to Alaska. But now…." He shook his head. "You're lucky Mulholland didn't bring you back in handcuffs."

"I remember, Simon."

"Remember what?"

"The weekend those two teachers went missing. Gina asked me to go out for dinner downtown. She picked me up. Said John was worried about me spending so much time alone when he was gone. And after she dropped me off that night, I never checked to see if my car was still in the garage. Why would I, right?"

Simon uncrossed his leg.

"I heard the garage door open when John got home from the airport in the middle of the night. And that must've been when you returned my Lexus."

Simon's expression soured, but he didn't bother denying it.

"When I found John," she continued, "there was a satellite phone on the counter in the cabin. I couldn't imagine who he would need to call after he made the world believe he was dead. Then I saw he'd been calling you every week. That you *knew*, this whole time, that he was alive. And *you* were the only witness to John's supposed bear attack."

Simon eyes pressed into hers. He leaned forward, resting his elbows on top of his knees. "What did you do, Cam?"

"You tell me, and I'll tell you."

Simon stood from the couch. "My involvement in his scheme happened slowly. When John first hinted to me that he was The Teacher Killer, I thought he was joking. Later, he showed me proof. I thought about turning him in, but he made me a better offer. You know how persuasive he could be. He knew that he couldn't get away with it forever. That it was only a matter of time before Mulholland tested that DNA from his first kill."

Simon abruptly stood and walked toward the kitchen. Cameron followed him to the back of the house. She eyed her cell phone, plugged in on the counter. Simon stopped to stare into her backyard through her French doors, though the daylight was all but gone.

"So, I agreed to help him capture those two women. In exchange for him mortgaging his home and faking his death to get the firm out of debt." He turned, and Cameron's eyes fell to the silver pistol in his hand. The one she'd given John for his forty-fifth birthday. The one he'd taken on his final hunt with Simon.

Her breath caught in her throat. She hadn't expected him to be armed. "Simon, please!"

He took a step toward her with the barrel of John's gun aimed at her heart.

She tore her eyes from the pistol and locked eyes with him. "How could you help him? You knew what he'd do to those women."

He sneered. "You're in no position to judge. You know what it's like to get away with murder. And I have proof." He reached inside his designer suit jacket and withdrew an SD card, housed in a plastic case. Just like the one in John's safety deposit box. "You didn't think John had the only copy, did you?"

Cameron swallowed. "You can't kill me. There's no way you'll get away with it."

He laughed. "You're unstable, Cam. All the evidence stacks up. You killed your first husband, and then you helped John get away with murder. And now that I've figured it out, you're trying to kill me."

He came another step closer. His cologne filled her nostrils. Cameron glanced at the gun, only inches from her chest.

I should've known. All this time, I should've known.

"Now," he said. "Tell me why John isn't answering his phone. Maybe, if you're truthful with me, I'll let you live. What happened, Cam?"

She locked her eyes with his. "The last time I saw John, he was still alive."

"When? Tell me the truth!"

She jumped from the ferocity of his voice. It triggered the memory of Miles's drunken rampages. She'd never seen Simon like this.

"Why do you care?"

"John's still my best friend. I've never met anyone like him." He raised the gun barrel toward her face. "What did you do to him, Cameron?"

"You're sick."

He pressed the barrel against her forehead. "Tell me."

She closed her eyes. This was the end. Maybe this was what she deserved for taking matters into her hands—twice. "I shot him. Then tied him to a tree outside the cabin. Then, Simon, I howled to draw in a rabid wolf pack before I left." She opened her eyelids to see Simon's lower lip quiver. "From the sounds of his screams, the wolves got to him before he froze."

"You ungrateful bitch."

Cameron stiffened as she braced for Simon to pull the trigger. In a rapid motion, Simon grabbed her hand and wrapped it around the pistol's handle. He turned it around, and Cameron tried to pull her hand away as he forced her finger onto the trigger.

The gun kicked as a blast resonated throughout the kitchen. Simon jerked backward from the shot to his shoulder. A grunt erupted from his throat as blood oozed through his dress shirt.

Cameron fought to wriggle her hand from the pistol, but Simon maintained his tight grip around hers.

"Simon!" she gasped. "What are you—"

"You shot me!" He turned the gun around and pressed the barrel against her breast. She gritted her teeth and strained to pull her pointer finger off the trigger.

"Simon, please! *Don't!*"

"You've given me no choice," he seethed.

His breath was warm against her face. She watched the traces of a smile reach the edge of his lips.

"It's self-defense." With everything he had, Simon pushed her finger against the trigger as a second shot rang out.

CHAPTER FORTY-SEVEN

"I'm here to see Simon Castelli." Tanner flashed his badge to the woman sitting behind a large marble desk at the entrance to the Castelli & Prescott downtown law firm.

He'd spent the last two days poring over Simon's—and the firm's—financial records, knowing he needed more evidence to prove that Simon was John's accomplice. Yesterday, he'd found the motive he'd been looking for. But before obtaining an arrest warrant, he was hoping to catch Simon in a lie—if not a confession.

"Oh, he's not here. He left about twenty minutes ago."

He looked out the fourteenth-floor window behind Simon's secretary at the sun setting behind the Olympic Mountains across the Sound. The view came with a lofty lease. "Do you know where he was headed?" His conversation with Simon's wife had led him to believe the attorney kept long hours at the office.

"I'm sorry, I don't." She reached for the phone near the corner of her desk. "But I can call him if you like?"

"No, that's okay. I'll try him at home."

Tanner hoped she wouldn't tip Simon off that he was looking for him as he rode the elevator to the parking garage. He wanted to catch Simon by surprise.

He crossed the parking area toward his Ford, thinking back to Simon explaining the law firm's financial troubles to Cameron in the interview room over a week ago. Simon told her that both he and John had taken out second mortgages to help the firm. Tanner knew Simon had only deposited two-hundred and fifty thousand, while John deposited a million. But Tanner assumed Simon couldn't leverage as much equity in his home. Until speaking to Gina and seeing Simon's extensive home remodel.

When he pulled Simon's financial records, he found there was no second mortgage on Simon's home. *And* he learned that Simon, being John's business partner, received a million-dollar life insurance payout last month. One that he failed to mention in his sob story to Cameron.

Tanner had also found a recent six-figure payment in Simon's bank account from a major television network. When he called them, he didn't get much out of the producer he spoke to, but enough to learn Simon was scheduled to do an exclusive interview about what it was like being John's business partner and long-time friend.

He opened the door to his Ford, wondering about the level of Simon's involvement in Alicia Lopez and Olivia Rossi's deaths. *Why would he help John kill?* He put his car into reverse and reflected on Simon being the only witness to John's bear attack that day in the Frank Church Wilderness. Did he blackmail John into taking out a million-dollar second mortgage? Had Simon killed him and made the whole thing up?

Three emergency tones came over his radio, interrupting his thoughts.

"Shots fired at 5501 Shoreline Drive, Seattle. Follow up on north radio."

Tanner turned on his lights and siren, pressing his foot on the gas as he pulled out of the parking garage, and sped toward Cameron's house.

CHAPTER FORTY-EIGHT

There was another blast of gunfire as Simon toppled against her, sending Cameron to the hardwood floor from the weight of his body. Cameron waited to feel the sting from the bullet when she realized that Simon wasn't moving.

A tall figure wearing a baseball cap stepped over them with a gun at his side. She screamed. *Had John somehow survived?*

"Cameron!" He kicked the gun out of Simon's reach before bending down and pushing Simon's limp body off hers.

She recognized Dane's voice at the same time her brain registered his face. "Are you okay?"

He helped her sit up. She grabbed his forearm. "How did you…?" She turned to Simon lying face-down on the floor. Blood pooled around the two bullet holes in his back. "Is he…is he dead?"

Dane reached out and placed his fingers against the side of Simon's neck. "No pulse."

Cameron scooted back as Simon's blood flowed toward her atop the hardwood floor. "We have to call the police."

She glanced at the SD card lying next to Simon's body. Dane's eyes followed hers. *How much had Dane heard?*

"Dane, what are you doing here?"

"When we came back to Tok from my lake cabin, there was a request and locate bulletin out for your Cessna. I heard it on my police scanner while you were tying up Karl's plane."

"Why didn't you say anything? Or arrest me?"

"There wasn't a warrant for your arrest. I thought the best thing for you would be to return home. I had Trooper Nelson leave the note in your room. But you stayed, and I wanted to know what you were doing in Tok. And why you seemed so interested in Bethany's murder. I wasn't planning on falling in love with you."

She searched his eyes.

"After you left like that, I needed to know where you went. So, I came here."

"John killed Bethany." She stared at Simon's lifeless form before turning back to Dane. "And I killed John."

"I heard."

If he was shocked, he didn't show it.

"But I didn't help John kill those women. I never knew."

"I know." He motioned to Simon's body. "He stole your car. I heard his whole confession."

"You did?"

He nodded. "Your front door was ajar, and I heard arguing. So, I let myself in."

She shook his arm. "Why did you wait? He could have killed me!"

"I'm sorry." He pointed back to the living room. "I didn't know he had a gun on you...until you told him about the wolves eating John." Cameron swallowed. Dane had also heard what she'd done to Miles. And knew there was evidence on the SD card to prove it.

Dane leaned forward and picked up the memory card. "I'll make the call," he said.

Her earlier relief was replaced by the fear of facing life imprisonment. She almost wished Dane had let Simon shoot her. Cameron accepted his hand and allowed him to pull her to her feet. "Are you going to give that to the police?"

She watched him pull his cell phone from his jacket pocket, feeling stupid for having asked. *Of course, he is. He's a cop.*

He hadn't come to rescue her. To learn she was a killer was a bonus to him.

He moved past her without a word and went to the kitchen sink. He turned the water on, dropped the card into the drain, and flipped the switch on the wall. The shrill sound of the garbage disposal grinding the electronic memory card drowned out the sirens in the distance. The Parkers had undoubtedly heard the shots.

Dane turned the disposal off. "There was no SD card. Understand?"

Was he helping her? Why?

He stepped out of the kitchen and came toward her. He pointed at Simon's body. "Cameron! Understand? He confessed to you that he was John's accomplice before he made it look like you shot him and then tried to kill you. I shot him before he pulled the trigger a second time. And that's all that happened." He put his hands on her shoulders and lowered his head until their eyes met. "Okay?"

She nodded.

He put his phone to his ear. "Yes, I have an emergency. I just witnessed an attempted murder. I've shot the perpetrator. We need an ambulance."

Cameron steadied herself against the counter as Dane made the 9-1-1 call. The room started to spin. Her breathing quickened as she watched Simon's face turn white. *Simon. How could you do this?*

She jumped from the weight of Dane's hand on her shoulder.

He lowered his phone to his side. "There was no SD card. Got it?"

She couldn't help but wonder if this was a trap. Was he working with Mulholland and trying to catch her in a lie?

She grabbed the front of Dane's coat. He didn't understand what she'd done. She wasn't some damsel in distress. "I killed someone."

He put his hand in the air. "I know. You told me."

Sirens wailed from outside as they came to a stop in front of her house.

She shook her head. "No, not John. A long time ago. I killed my ex-husband. He was beating me. It's what was on that SD card. I made it look like a sui—"

He stepped toward her and put his palms on either side of her face. "I heard. I know. And someday, you can tell me the whole story, but not tonight."

Her front door flew open. A uniformed officer stormed inside alongside Mulholland, guns drawn. "Police! Hands on your head!"

CHAPTER FORTY-NINE

Alone in the tiny interview room at Seattle Homicide, Cameron stared at the grey squares of acoustic foam adhered to the top of the walls. Mulholland had already questioned her about what happened at her home. When he stood to leave, he had asked if she'd found what she was looking for in Alaska.

"John is dead. I know that now."

He had told her to wait while he spoke with Dane, but that was over half an hour ago. For the first few minutes, she'd strained to hear what they were saying on the other side of the wall, but the soundproofing made it impossible.

She leaned back in the metal chair. *What was Dane telling him? Everything?* Maybe she'd been a fool to trust him. She didn't exactly have a great track record for picking men.

The door to the interview room swung open. Mulholland had a folder in his hand, which he slapped atop the small table before sitting across from her. He chewed a piece of gum in the side of his mouth that hadn't been there when they last spoke.

Cameron straightened. Mulholland cleared his throat.

"You left Tok six days ago. What took you so long to get back?"

"I had an errand to run."

He raised his eyebrows. "An errand? Care to elaborate?"

Cameron shook her head.

He chewed his gum. "Okay. But while you're here…there's something else I'd like to ask you about."

He opened the folder and spun it around. Her eyes fell to the photo on top. She recognized it immediately. She looked away.

Had Dane betrayed her?

"I apologize that these images may be hard to see. But there's some things that don't add up about your first husband's suicide." Mulholland pointed to the picture. "You see how the gun is still in his grip even though he's slumped forward on the couch? From the angle of his body, I would've expected his arm to fall forward and then the gun to slip from his hand. It seems unnatural for his arm to have landed this way."

Cameron forced herself to look at Miles's charred remains. *He never saw it coming.* Miles was four beers in—watching football—when she had snuck up behind him, wearing her yellow kitchen gloves, and shot him in the temple with his own gun.

He slumped forward and she grabbed the back of his shirt to keep him from falling off the couch. She examined the hole in the side of his head, seeping with blood and tissue, surprised to find she felt nothing. Then, she'd placed the pistol in his grip, bending his elbow so the gun stayed on his lap. After dousing the room with gasoline, she placed the gas can near Miles's feet. She made sure she'd soaked the cupboard with fuel before returning her gloves to the cabinet beneath the kitchen sink.

She ran to her room and changed clothes—in case of any splatter—before using a lighter to ignite the fuel around Miles's body.

She fled the house and calmly purchased beer and milk at the nearby convenience store before returning home, relieved to see the house was engulfed in flames. She would never forget how black the smoke was.

"According to Miles's autopsy report, he died before inhaling any smoke, which means he would've had to start the fire at almost the exact same time he shot himself."

She tore her eyes from the photo and met Mulholland's eyes.

"You were conveniently gone from the home when all this happened," he continued. "And strangely, a woman recently called the Sequim gas station that you visited a week before Miles died and asked about their surveillance footage from eleven years ago."

Cameron flipped the manila folder closed.

"I went to Sequim and spoke with Tina, the hygienist who used to work for you. She thought Miles was abusing you." He folded his hands. "Is there anything you want to tell me?"

She pushed the folder to his side of the table. "Have you ever had to live in fear of the person you lived with? *Real* fear.

Be terrorized by the person who vowed to cherish and protect you? Do you know what that's like?"

"No, I have not."

"Well, I can tell you. It's like living in a war zone. Except you're unarmed. At least at first, they feel like surprise attacks. You have no warning of when they might happen or what might trigger them."

He sat completely still, waiting for her to go on.

"Then, you find yourself constantly on edge. Bracing yourself for the next assault. Your partner raises his voice, and you feel yourself flinch. You're afraid that if you leave, you'll be found. And if you stay, you will die.

"While I was married to Miles, I heard a war veteran liken his PTSD to zombies. Like zombies, traumatic experiences can eat you alive. And pop up when you least expect them. That was living with Miles."

"So, what did you do?"

Cameron held his gaze. "I didn't have to do anything. Miles killed *himself*. As tragic as that is, I guess I should consider myself fortunate."

Tanner's eyes searched hers as his jaw flexed from his gum. Some people were better liars than others. And Cameron showed all the signs of telling the truth. If he didn't know better, he would have believed her.

"I guess so." He thanked her for answering his questions before he stood from the table.

"Of course."

Cameron went out the door he held open for her. He escorted her to the elevator, where the Alaskan state trooper was waiting. After the doors closed on the two of them, Mulholland went back to his desk. It was after midnight, but there were two other detectives still working.

He grabbed Miles Henson's thin case file and absently flipped through it. It was strange that the state trooper had followed Cameron home. When he questioned him, the trooper said he was concerned for her after Cameron left Tok and he couldn't reach her by phone. He figured she'd come back to Seattle, and he decided to check on her in person.

But Tanner suspected there was more to it than that. He had an inkling the trooper wasn't being completely honest with him. He guessed the trooper had feelings for Cameron. Or could his interest in her be something else?

The detectives in the adjacent cubicle turned off their desk lights. Tanner leaned back in his chair.

"Hey, Mulholland. You wanna tear yourself away and join us for a beer?" one of them asked. "Might be good for you."

He stared at Miles Henson's burnt remains before closing the case file. "Yeah, I could use one." He pulled on his coat. After dropping the contents of Henson's case file into the paper shredder, he followed them out of the unit. "First round's on me."

CHAPTER FIFTY

Three Months Later

Cameron looked out the windshield of her Cessna at the rugged terrain north of Tok. The snow had thawed, and Hunt Lake glimmered a vibrant blue among the green forest that surrounded it.

"Beautiful day for a flight," she said into her mouthpiece.

"I've been too busy admiring the pilot to notice." Dane's eyes moved to her freshly dyed red hair. "I'm glad you decided to stay a redhead. It suits you."

A dimple appeared on the side of his cheek when he smiled at her. Her eyes fell to his bicep that protruded beneath his grey t-shirt and she forced her attention to return to the surrounding skies.

After a thorough investigation, no charges had been brought against Dane—or Cameron—in Simon's death. And Mulholland held a press conference announcing that Simon was being posthumously charged with being an accomplice in the murders of Alicia Lopez and Olivia Rossi.

In the days following Simon's death, she'd told Dane everything she'd planned on keeping secret for the rest of her life. Instead of turning her in, he'd listened—without judgment—astonished that she'd made the trek to Miles's cabin in the middle of winter, on her own.

After the sale of her Laurelhurst home—and John's Cle Elum cabin, she'd purchased a quaint two-story home in the woods outside of town, on a property close to Dane. She'd taken over the small dental practice in Tok after the town's dentist retired last month.

It was still agonizing for them to see Bethany and Grace's parents around town, but at least Dane and Cameron had the peace of knowing John was dead. Maybe, someday, they would find a way to tell the girls' parents.

"Look." Dane pointed out the window.

Cameron sat up straight and looked below. A brown bear and her cub moved slowly along an opening in the trees.

"Amazing." Seeing Alaskan wildlife in their natural habitat was something she wasn't sure she would ever get used to.

Her thoughts wandered to John after seeing the bears. She looked beyond the window at the Yukon-Charley Rivers area in the distance, near the horizon. Dane squeezed her hand.

She wondered if any of John's remains were still out there. Cameron looked one last time in the direction of Miles's family cabin before banking and turning back for Tok.

EPILOGUE

Tanner pushed himself through the last mile of his early morning run on the beachside path at Lincoln Park. The late spring rain came down hard, but over the years he'd lived in Seattle, he had learned to enjoy his runs no matter what the weather. He picked up his pace as he followed the path along the water.

In the months since Simon Castelli was killed, his mind kept going back to Cameron's time in Alaska. Before she left, she was in denial about John's death. But by the time she returned, she'd told him with absolute certainty that John was gone. And he needed to know why.

After the news of John's bear attack, he'd been convinced John died in the Frank Church Wilderness. But now that he knew Simon was an unreliable witness by being complicit in John's crimes, he wondered if there was some validity to Cameron's doubts about John's death. He'd already contacted Alaska's Department of Natural Resources and been assured that neither John nor Simon owned any properties within the state. Interestingly, the search pulled up a new record: Cameron had recently settled down in Tok.

As he watched the Vashon Island ferry pull away from the pier, he considered one last possible angle. He sprinted the last half mile until he reached the parking lot.

Tanner called his contact at the Alaska Department of Natural Resources the moment he got to his desk. It wasn't yet seven a.m. in Anchorage, so he left a voicemail asking them to call him back as soon as possible.

Two hours later, he recognized the 907-area code on his call ID. He answered after the first ring.

"Hey, I need you to search for another name for me. Miles Christopher Henson. I can give you his social security number."

"Okay, give me just a second while I run that through our database." The woman came back on less than a minute later. "Okay, so nothing came up under Miles, but I've got a property belonging to an Andrew Christopher Henson. It's inside the Yukon-Charly Rivers National Preserve, which means it can't be sold, but it can be handed down through the family. It looks like Andrew Henson purchased the property in 1947, thirty years before the national preserve was established."

"Can you email me the property address and that information?"

"Yes, of course. I'll send it to you now."

Tanner hung up and waited an agonizing minute for the email to land in his inbox. He opened it as soon as it appeared. After copying the property address, he pasted it into an online map.

Staring at the red dot that appeared halfway between Fairbanks and the Canadian border, he pulled a fresh stick of gum from his pocket and folded it into his mouth.

WANT MORE?

Get your FREE bonus content and new release updates at
AUDREYJCOLE.com/sign-up

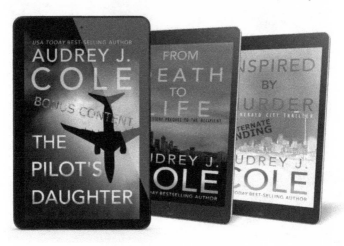

ACKNOWLEDGEMENTS

Huge thanks to my editor, Bryan Tomasovich, for your tireless work, guidance, and mostly, for introducing me to ice fishing.

Special thanks to my agent, Jill Marsal, for your impeccable judgment and thoughtful advocacy.

Thanks to Penny Lane for helping me fine-tune my manuscript by seeing what I can't.

To Seattle Homicide Detective Rolf Norton, thank you for taking the time once again to help me better understand the incredible work that you do.

To Alaska State Troopers Cody Webb, Jaimie Burnham, and Russel Landers, thank you for inviting me into your station in Tok and giving me a firsthand look at how you operate. And to Corporal Dan Teel, thank you for explaining your work in Alaska and answering my procedural questions.

To Clay Richmond, thanks for sharing your wealth of knowledge and fascinating stories about wolves. Without you, Cameron would never have known how to howl to draw them in.

Thank you to Jenifer Ruff, Tim and Julie Browne, and Chris Patchell for your input and friendship.

To my family, thank you for your endless support, encouragement, and putting up with my obsession over my stories.

Thank you to all my readers—I couldn't do this without you. Hearing that you've enjoyed my books means the world to me.

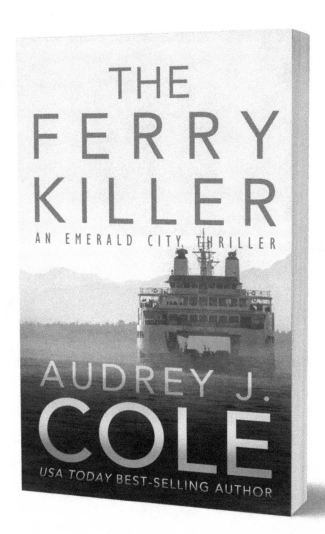

COMING 2023

START THE EMERALD CITY THRILLER SERIES TODAY

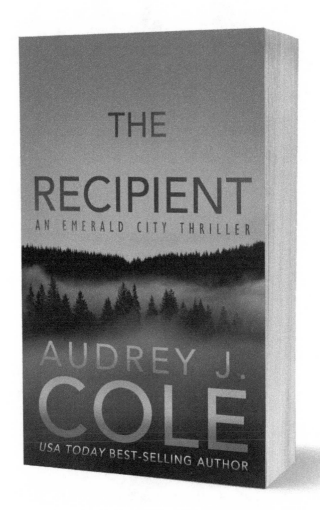

THE RECIPIENT

CHAPTER ONE

Samantha walked barefoot down the vacated hallway to the ice machine, just a few doors down from her lavish hotel room. The carpet felt good on her feet after wearing new high heels in and out of meetings all day.

Although tired, she couldn't complain. The investment company she worked for had put her up in a plush hotel during her three-day Seattle business trip. Knowing how unstable the economy had been over the last decade made her thankful to have landed such a prestigious job right out of college.

She reached the ice machine and looked down at the gleaming diamond ring she wore on her left hand. It reminded her that she only had two more weeks to plan the final details before she tied the knot with Harrison, her boyfriend of three years. She smiled to herself as she envisioned the intimate ceremony that would take place in her hometown of Denver, Colorado. Their outdoor reception would have the beautiful backdrop of the Rocky Mountains. She placed the ice bucket under the spout, which muffled the noise of footsteps coming up behind her.

Samantha gasped and dropped her ice bucket when she felt a firm hand on her shoulder. She turned to see an attractive man smiling at her.

"I'm sorry, I didn't mean to scare you," he said, kneeling to lift the bucket from the floor. "I just figured you wouldn't be able to hear me over the ice machine."

He handed her back the bucket and proceeded to grab the few pieces of ice that had escaped onto the woven carpet before standing up.

"I seem to have lost my room key, and I was wondering if I might use the phone in your room to call the front desk," he said, taking a step toward her.

He was good-looking and probably just trying to pick her up, but she didn't like the way he was intruding on her personal space. The man looked to be in his mid-thirties. Like her, he was dressed in business attire, but his worn-in baseball hat looked out of place. She noticed his jacket also looked way too casual to be worn over a dress shirt and tie.

"Why don't you just go down to the front desk and get a new key?" Samantha took a step back, uncomfortable with his request and his proximity to her in the empty hallway.

Seeing her apprehension, the man's smile faded. He took a quick look behind him as if to make sure they were still alone in the hall, and she began to think she might be in danger.

"Oh, right. I'll just do that." His expression turned cold and he lingered for an uncomfortable moment.

She knew she might be imagining it, but she could see evil in his eyes as he stared at her. She took another step back and wondered if she should cry out for help before he turned and walked away. She watched him move down the hallway and let out the breath she'd been holding in.

Once he was out of her sight, she finished filling the ice bucket. She looked over her shoulder to make sure he was gone before taking quick steps back to her room.

She still had the man on her mind when she got back to her door and realized her room key was no longer in her hand. She was sure she had taken it with her. *It must've fallen when I dropped the ice bucket.* She swore under her breath, ready to be back inside the safety of her room.

Begrudgingly, she started back toward the ice machine when she saw her keycard on the floor right in front of her door. *Thank goodness.* She picked it up, opened her door, and went inside. She made sure it had completely closed behind her before she turned the lock and set the latch as an extra precaution.

Her iPhone rang and she set the bucket down on her nightstand before pulling the phone out of her purse. *Harrison.* She stretched out on the pillow top mattress and felt herself relax from the sound of his voice. They didn't talk for long. She could hardly keep her eyes open while she reclined on the comfortable bed and spoke to her fiancé.

After they hung up, she laid her phone down and wandered into the bathroom to wash her face. She pulled her curly red hair into a bun atop her head. The moment she splashed her face with water, she heard something squeak. She assumed it came from the room next to her and continued to wash off her makeup when an electric current surged through her body. She arched her back in response to the pain. She started to cry out but fell silent as her body convulsed from the shock. The muscles in her legs gave out, and she dropped to the tile floor.

Her vision was blurred from the makeup remover and mascara running into her eyes, but she recognized the man from the ice machine standing over her. He held a black object in one of his gloved hands and what looked like a needle and syringe in the other. She felt a rush of panic and scrambled to get up, but her muscles were too weak from the shock.

The man knelt beside her and set the black object down on the tile. Her breathing quickened as he clamped his gloved hand around her wrist. He jabbed the inside of her arm with the needle and plunged the contents of the syringe into one of her antecubital veins. He calmly recapped the needle after removing it from her arm.

Some of her strength returned. She managed to sit up and push herself against the bathroom wall. Her vision had cleared, and she watched the man pick the black object up off the floor. She started to let out a scream but was brought to silence when another electric current ripped through her body.

She fell to the side. Her head smacked against the floor. Before her muscles had time to recover from the shock, the man pressed his gloved hand hard over her mouth. He leaned his face down close to hers. He held what she now knew to be a Taser up in front of her face.

"I'll use this as many times as I have to, so it's up to you how much pain you want to go through." His voice was calm but authoritative at the same time. His confidence made her more afraid than anything else. "Do you understand?"

He moved the Taser closer to her face. She nodded.

"Good."

He pulled her to her feet while keeping his hand tightly clamped over her mouth. Samantha stared at their reflection in the mirror. Her handsome attacker stood behind her. Black streaks of mascara ran down her face.

He laid the Taser down on the counter and she knew this might be her only chance. She thrashed back and forth, using all her strength to try and get away from him. He fell against the towel rack but managed to keep his hand over her mouth. Her heart felt as if it would beat through her chest as she watched him lift up a large knife in his other hand. He held the knife less than an inch away from her face.

"We can do this the easy way or the hard way, it's up to you."

She felt the warmth of his breath as he whispered in her ear.

Fear mounted inside her as she stared at the double-edged knife. Filled with a sense of impending doom, she allowed herself to lessen her resistance against his hold. She could only imagine what he had planned for her.

She felt sick to her stomach as she watched him grin at her in the mirror. Her hair had come loose from her bun and now fell in a mess around her face. He used the tip of the blade to tuck her hair back behind her ear and leaned in closer.

"That's better."

She closed her eyes as he started to sing the lyrics to "Killing Me Softly."

ABOUT THE AUTHOR

Audrey J. Cole is a *USA TODAY* bestselling thriller author. She resides in the Pacific Northwest with her husband and two children. Before writing full time, she worked as a neonatal intensive care nurse for eleven years.

Connect with Audrey:

f facebook.com/AudreyJCole

BB bookbub.com/authors/Audrey-J-Cole

instagram.com/AudreyJCole/

You can also visit her website:

www.AUDREYJCOLE.com